GHOST TOWNING

FOR
FUN, ADVENTURE, AND DISCOVERY

CAPTAIN S. MARTIN SHELTON, USNR (RET.)

Inquiries should be addressed to the Publisher:
Lamplight Press
PO Box 82516,
Austin, Texas 78708

First Printing 2017

ISBN: 978-0-9892861-9-0

Printed in the United States of America

TABLE OF CONTENTS

DEDICATION

I dedicate this publication to the late Doctor Donald E. Pickart. Don was my friend for 45 years and he accompanied me on many of my ghost town trips.

ACKNOWLEDGMENTS

I'm indebted to many folks who helped me in preparation of this book. And without whose valuable assistance this book would not have been written and published.

Those who ventured with me exploring the wilds are Ken Albright, Jack Lyons, Ron Maryott, Jr., George McCormick, and Donald Thompson. Intrepid ghost-towners all.

Danielle H. Acee, Lamplight Press, for her outstanding work in formatting this manuscript and herding it through the publication process.

Marta Galvan who did the first-cut editing of this publication with her eagle-eyes.

Ron James, former Nevada State Historic Preservation Officer, Carson City Nevada; for his expert counsel and sterling support.

K.C. Francis for her final draft editing.

LIST OF ILLUSTRATIONS

GHOST TOWN PHOTOGRAPHIC GALLERY

At the conclusion of each chapter, I included several photographs of ghost towns that are scattered throughout our many Western states. In Chapter Seventeen, I've included a potpourri of scenic sites.

Chp. 1. Tenabo, NV; Masonic Lodge, Hamilton, NV
         Ophir, NV; Grafton, UT
         Atolia, CA; Grafton, UT
         Old Nye County Court House, Belmont, NV; Mariscal Mecury Mine, TX

Chp. 2. Lochiel, AZ; Abo, NM
         Grafton, UT; US Land Office, Bodie, CA
         Paria, UT; Aguilar, CO
         Belmont Mill, NV; Langtry, TX

Chp. 3. Strozzi Ranch, NV; Cerritos, NM
         Swansea, AZ; Methodist Church, Bodie, CA
         Dryden, TX; Belmont, NV
         Gold Spring, UT; Orla, TX

Chp. 4. Bruncaw, AZ; Delamar, NV
         Odd Fellows' Lodge and Miner's Union Hall, Bodie, CA; Carrara, NV
         Ancho, NM; Ione, NV
         Little Daisy Hotel, Jerome, AZ; Ryan, CA

Chp. 5. Chemung Mine, CA; Abandoned Machinery, Hamilton, NV
         Valedon, NM; Pontotoc, TX
         Grantsville, NV; Penwell, TX
         James Stuart House, Bodie, CA; Sasco, AZ

Chp. 6. Bodie School, CA; Pueblo, TX
         Barstow, TX; Ruby, AZ
         Ballarat, CA; Winter Ranch, NV
         Jerome, AZ; Schoolhouse, Kent, TX

viii

Moapa, NV; Pat Reddy's House, Bodie, CA
Opera House, Hamilton, NV; Cow Camp, Hyde Well, NV

Chp. 16. Betty O'Neal Mine, NV; Withington Hotel, Hamilton, NV
Highbridge Mill, NV; Berlin, NV
Ludwick, NV; Belmont Mill, NV
Schoolhouse, Rhyolite, NV; Minerva, NV

Chp. 17. Scenics, listed in sequence.
- "Quaking Aspens," Shoshone Mountains, NV
- Guadalupe Mountains National Park, TX
- "Quaking Aspens," Siegel Creek, NV
- "Approaching Winter Storm," Highway 50, Big Smoky Valley, NV
- Coral Pink Sand Dunes State Park, UT
- "Pecan Trees," Jonah, TX
- Beowawe Cemetery, Eureka County, NV
- "My Blazer," Cottonwood Canyon, NV
- Onion Creek, Dripping Springs, TX
- Oasis Valley, Nye County, NV
- "Split-rail Fence," Fredericksburg, TX
- "Quaking Aspens," Paradise Valley, NV
- "Wildflowers" at the Cotton Mill, Walberg, TX
- "Forest Home," Garden Valley, NV
- "Lone Cabin," Panguitch, UT
- "Red Door," Holland, TX

PREFACE

The ghost towns of the American West have a historic lure for the adventurous, explorers, academics, and photographers. For over a century, the romantic mystique of the westward migration has captured our rustic imagination: wagon trains, gold rushes, gunfights, bawdy saloons, and all the melodramatic characters therein. We satiate our curiosity through novels, film, television, games, and by taking trips to these remote regions to savor their storied ambiance. Yet, we must understand that these ghost towns, precious remnants of our past, are fragile and non-renewable resources. They are vulnerable to a harsh environment, artifact collectors, and lawless vandals, all of which have done incredible damage to these sites. Enjoy your visits and be an assiduous conservator to protect them—take out everything you brought to the site and leave everything that you did not bring to it.

There are strict federal and state laws protecting our ghost towns. Yet, some folks ignore those laws to satisfy their illegal and untoward activities: serious looting, senseless damage, and infantile graffiti. I've seen it all, and then some. Once a ghost town is sacked, it's lost forever.

CHAPTER ONE

INTRODUCTION

Scattered throughout the Western states are a plethora of ghost towns. A few sites are nearly complete towns—and for many others, all that remains is a hole in the ground and two tin cans, if anything. In between, lay sites of all sizes, conditions, and accessibility. I use the all-inclusive "ghost town" to include abandoned (or nearly abandoned) towns, mining camps, military outposts, stagecoach stations, deserted ranches, and farms. Unfortunately, vandals, time, wildfires, and the vagaries of weather are taking their toll on these historic sites. In just a few years, some have changed drastically due to these negative elements.

For the adventurous, ghost towning is a daunting challenge in exploration and hearty satisfaction in discovery. It's an excellent opportunity for photographers to exercise their artistic talent to get that "great shot." My purpose here is to provide a comprehensive guide to the process of ghost towning—how to's, don'ts, guides, cautions, and tips. I do not delve into the history of these sites—that's beyond the scope of this publication and my capabilities. Several excellent books detail the history of the ghost towns of the West (see bibliography).

In forty-nine trips over thirty-one years, I've photographed about 2,000 sites in our Western states—including many that were lost to history. I focused my ghost towning activities in Nevada, California, Arizona, New Mexico, Texas, and a few sites in Utah and Colorado. My goal was to find the sites and to document them with photography, and to prepare a written description detailing what remains there: structures, equipment, geographic description, flora, environment, and hazards. Critical to this documentation was determining the sites' precise location. To this end, I used a Global Positioning System device. Prior to my onsite visits, I researched the literature, studied U. S. Geological Survey (USGS) topographic maps to plan my routes to the sites, and consulted other sources of information. On the whole, it took me one day of planning for one day in the field.

Tenabo, NV
Date of Photograph: 4 September, 1991
Ghost Town Rating: 6
Road Condition Rating: 2

Masonic Lodge, Hamilton, NV
Date of Photograph: 23 October, 1994
Ghost Town Rating: 8
Road Condition Rating: 3

Murphy Mine and Mill, Ophir, NV
Date of Photograph: 5 November, 1992
Ghost Town Rating: 8
Road Condition Rating: 5

Grafton, UT
Date of Photograph: 24 October, 1996
Ghost Town Rating: 8
Road Condition Rating: 2

Atolia, CA
Date of Photograph: 27 December, 1997
Ghost Town Rating: 8
Road Condition Rating: 1

Grafton, UT
Date of Photograph: 24 October, 1996
Ghost Town Rating: 8
Road Condition Rating: 2

Old Nye County Court House, Belmont, NV
Date of Photograph: 18 November, 1989
Ghost Town Rating: 9
Road Condition Rating: 1

Mariscal Mercury Mine, TX
Date of Photograph: 12 July, 2013
Ghost Town Rating: 7
Road Condition Rating: 3

Chapter Two

Protocols

Don't be a **vandal**, or in the vernacular, a "bottle digger." When you visit a ghost town, it's incumbent on you to abide by federal and state laws regarding protection of archaeological resources and private property. In essence, we're morally and legally obligated to scrupulously adhere to "ghost town etiquette:"

Take out everything you bring in and take out nothing you didn't bring in.

Following this etiquette allows others to discover the beauty and mystery of these fragile historic sites. They are, in fact, nonrenewable resources. They are antiquities.

There are several federal laws governing the protection of archaeological resources (antiquities) on federal land. In Nevada, the federal government owns 83% of the land—administered by the Bureau of Land Management. Of primary interest is The Archaeological Resources Protection Act of 1979; Title 16 U.S. Code, Paragraph 470. This Act details prohibited activities regarding antiquities; for example, the unauthorized removal, destruction, excavation, damage, etc. to archaeological sites; and it describes the criminal and civil penalties for violations. This act also discusses topics such as interstate trafficking in antiquities and enforcement procedures.

Should you have any doubts about how serious the federal authorities are about this law, then I urge you to read the Act carefully and heed it assiduously. You can find the complete Act on the Internet or in your local library. I'll share just one example of some folks who were successfully prosecuted for violation of this Federal law. In 1988, Forest Service Law Enforcement Officers cited two fellows for vandalizing the Shermantown site in White Pine County. They were caught selling artifacts they uncovered at the site: coins, bottles, and such. Their lawyer plea-bargained the charge from a felony to a misdemeanor under the Code of Federal Regulations (36 CFR 2610), theft and destruction of federal property. The cost to these culprits was a fine, lawyer's fees, court costs, lost time, and a record of this conviction with the U.S. Forest Service.

I'll summarize: **leave your metal detector at home.**

Do not enter private property without permission. I urge you to be equally circumspect with antiquities located on that property. If not, you could be charged under state laws with trespassing, theft, and destruction of private property.

Last item on this topic: if you spot someone vandalizing a site, notify federal authorities or the local sheriff. Do not attempt to apprehend or curtail their activities. Doing so could be dangerous to you and your party.

CAUTION. Several historic sites are located within the boundaries of the Department of Defense and Department of Energy restricted facilities. Under no conditions attempt to enter these areas. It's dangerous, you could compromise national security, and you'll probably get arrested. Such is especially the case with the Air Force's Nellis Test Range (Area 51). This is a high-security area and unauthorized personnel are not allowed access. Don't bother to ask. Signs posted throughout this area warn that lethal force may be used on intruders. 'Nuff said.

I don't mean to sound preachy. But, I'm dedicated to preserving these sites and I want you and your children, their children, and their children to savor the nostalgia of these wonderful sites for as long as we can.

Lochiel, AZ
Date of Photograph: 5 November, 2005
Ghost Town Rating: 7
Road Condition Rating: 2

Abo, NM
Date of Photograph: 8 October, 2007
Ghost Town Rating: 3
Road Condition Rating: 2

Grafton, UT
Date of Photograph: 24 October, 1996
Ghost Town Rating: 8
Road Condition Rating: 2

US Land Office, Bodie, CA
Date of Photograph: 1 August, 1981
Ghost Town Rating: 10
Road Condition Rating: 2

Paria, UT
Date of Photograph: 27 September, 1992
Ghost Town Rating: 8
Road Condition Rating: 3

Aguilar, CO
Date of Photograph: 13 October, 1997
Ghost Town Rating: 3
Road Condition Rating: 1

Belmont Mill, NV
Date of Photograph: 24 October, 1993
Ghost Town Rating: 7
Road Condition Rating: 4

Langtry, TX
Date of Photograph: 19 July, 2008
Ghost Town Rating: 8
Road Condition Rating: 1

CHAPTER THREE

HISTORIC SITE RATING SYSTEM

I rated the various sites pictured in this document according to the quality and quantity of what remains. My ratings are based on the conditions I saw on the day I visited the site. Such conditions may not exist (probably will not) in the future.

I rated the sites on a scale of 0 to 10. Five is the average (defined below). Factors I considered in assigning a rating to a site included: number of structures, their condition, types, size, etc.; size of the site area; and to a lesser degree the amount and type of equipment, junk, and stuff scattered about.

I defined structures to include man-made things, such as buildings (single and multi-story), houses, huts, corrals, windmills, foundations, kilns, chimneys, stone- or brick-lined pits, mills, head frames, and related structures. Roads were specifically excluded and are discussed in Chapter Seven.

Though I defined the quality of each site in discrete terms by assigning it a definitive number, please understand that in reality the rating scale is a continuum of quality that ranges from nothing to the best, 0 to 10. The rating numbers are interim measures on this continuum.

Also, the definitions I gave to the rating numbers have wide latitude in interpretation. It's nearly impossible to define each rating number with pinpoint precision. Nonetheless, in each definition I gave typical scenarios of what's at that type of site. It could be more, or less, of the same or different stuff.

Clearly, such a rating system is subjective and has a built-in bias, which could influence my ratings by a factor of plus or minus one (+/- 1). Also influencing my rating system were special conditions found at the sites, for instance, extensive ruins and paraphernalia scattered over a wide area and no complete structure standing probably would cause me to upgrade the site one number.

Not all of the sites are absolute "ghost towns"—that is, not totally abandoned. Some sites are marginally functioning towns in which ruins remain as a reminder of their past larger size. One such site is Manhattan in Nye County. Some other sites, though not functioning towns, have a few inhabitants; for example, Belmont, Nye County.

Site Rating System

0. A site but nothing remains; for example, Round Spring, White Pine County.
1. Minimal evidence of a site, such as scattered tin cans, boards, or a hole in the ground; for example, Sarcobatus, Esmeralda County, Nevada.
2. Enough man-made stuff to firmly establish the site. Standing structures, if any, are minimal in quality and quantity, such as a framed mine entrance, a loader in poor condition, or a foundation; for example, Monarch, Nye County.
3. Collapsed ruins of a structure or two, such as a low, partial standing wall, no roof; mining equipment, considerable detritus about, perhaps a corral, windmill, and a fence; for example, Reveille, Nye County.

4. One or two structures, one may have a partial roof; extensive debris scattered about; mining equipment, well, corral; for example, Sylvania, Esmeralda County. Or, a complete structure in reasonably good condition with a nearly complete roof plus remnants of other structures; for example, Stone House, White Pine County.

5. Two or three standing structures, one has a nearly complete roof. Generally such structures are in poor to fair condition. There may be the remains of collapsed structures on the ground. Other man-made stuff is about; for example, Henry, Elko County.

6. Two or three standing structures, at least one has a complete roof, others may have partial or no roofs; at least one of the structures in middling condition; or a moderately sized mining or processing facility and related equipment; for example, Cortez, Lander County.

7. Three or more standing structures, several of which are in fair condition, spread over an extensive area; several stone walls of varying heights, remnants of other stone buildings, large mining and ore processing facilities; for example, Grand Deposit, White Pine County.

8. Several standing structures, some with complete roofs. Structures cover a moderately large area; condition ranges from fair to good; extensive remnants of other structures abound including, perhaps, remains of a multistory structure. Lots of "stuff" about (automobiles, mining equipment, and man-made junk); for example, Hamilton, Nevada.

9. Many standing structures in fair to good condition, other structures or partial structures ranging from poor to fair. A multi-story structure and/or remains of multi-story structures in poor to fair condition. Site covers a wide area; for example, Belmont, Nye County.

10. An entire large town, with a dozen or more structures in generally fair to excellent condition. Such structures are made of wood, brick, and cinder blocks and most have whole roofs. There are several multi-story structures in good condition. A few structures vary from poor to fair, but on the whole, the overall condition is superior. May have extensive mining equipment and other stuff scattered about. A large mine with several buildings may be associated with the site. The only site I'd have assigned the grade of 10 to is Bodie, Mono County, California—a State Park.

Strozzi Ranch, NV
Date of Photograph: 1 March, 1998
Ghost Town Rating: 7
Road Condition Rating: 4

Cerritos, NM
Date of Photograph: 13 October, 2007
Ghost Town Rating: 4
Road Condition Rating: 1

Swansea, AZ
Date of Photograph: 13 November, 2006
Ghost Town Rating: 3
Road Condition Rating: 2

Methodist Church, Bodie, CA
Date of Photograph: 1 August, 1981
Ghost Town Rating: 10
Road Condition Rating: 2

Dryden, TX
Date of Photograph: 16 November, 2005
Ghost Town Rating: 4
Road Condition Rating: 1

Belmont, NV
Date of Photograph: 19 November, 1989
Ghost Town Rating: 9
Road Condition Rating: 1

Gold Spring, UT
Date of Photograph: 24 October, 1996
Ghost Town Rating: 5
Road Condition Rating: 4

Orla, TX
Date of Photograph: 15 April, 2012
Ghost Town Rating: 8
Road Condition Rating: 1

CHAPTER FOUR

ALSO KNOWN AS (AKA) NAMES

Many ghost towns in the West have alternate names or variations in spelling. For example, about 35 percent of the sites in Nevada fit this category. One example is Bonnie Claire in Nye County. This site has five alternate names (Clare, Clair, Thorps, Thorp Wells, and Montana Station). For additional information, I would suggest that you consult Shawn Hall's excellent Nevada ghost town books. They are listed in the Bibliography.

The primary site name I used in my work is the name printed on the USGS topographic maps. If the USGS map did not spot a site, then I used the name that I saw most often in the research material. When I found a site that was not spotted on the maps or mentioned in the literature, then I dubbed the site "Ruins" and added the nearest topographic name on the topographic map. For example, "Ruins, Parther Springs," in Elko County, Nevada.

Bruncaw, AZ
Date of Photograph: 4 November, 2005
Ghost Town Rating: 3
Road Condition Rating: 3

Delamar, NV
Date of Photograph: 23 October, 1995
Ghost Town Rating: 8
Road Condition Rating: 3

Odd Fellows' Lodge, and Miner's Union Hall, Bodie, CA
Date of Photograph: 1 August, 1981
Ghost Town Rating: 10
Road Condition Rating: 2

Carrara, NV
Date of Photograph: 23 October, 1995
Ghost Town Rating: 6
Road Condition Rating: 3

Ancho, NM
Date of Photograph: 21 October, 2002
Ghost Town Rating: 8
Road Condition Rating: 1

Ione, NV
Date of Photograph: 17 November, 1989
Ghost Town Rating: 6
Road Condition Rating: 3

Little Daisy Hotel, Jerome, AZ
Date of Photograph: 7 November, 2005
Ghost Town Rating: 8
Road Condition Rating: 1

Ryan, CA
Date of Photograph: 24 February, 1991
Ghost Town Rating: 8
Road Condition Rating: 2

CHAPTER FIVE

MAPS AND LATITUDE AND LONGITUDE

Throughout my documentation of historic ghost towns, I detailed their locations using the time-tested measure of *latitude* and *longitude*. Simply, latitude and longitude are two-dimensional metrics by which any place on our planet can be located to within an accuracy of 101 square feet. Nowadays, the signals from the geospatial satellites can define these measures to an exceptionally fine degree, giving dimensions having an accuracy of two or three decimal points. Accordingly, we can define the location of any spot on the planet's surface to within a few square feet. For those who want more technical information, please consult an encyclopedia and a spherical trigonometry book.

Here's the background. At the International Meridian Conference in Washington, D.C., in 1884, world governments agreed on a universal system of global measurements—essential for precision navigation at the time. The mathematics of the spherical trigonometry involved is abstruse. No need to get that involved here. Let's keep our discussion fundamental.

Latitude is a series of imaginary lines that circle our planet and are parallel to the equator. These lines define positions in the north and south directions in terms of degrees (as in angles).

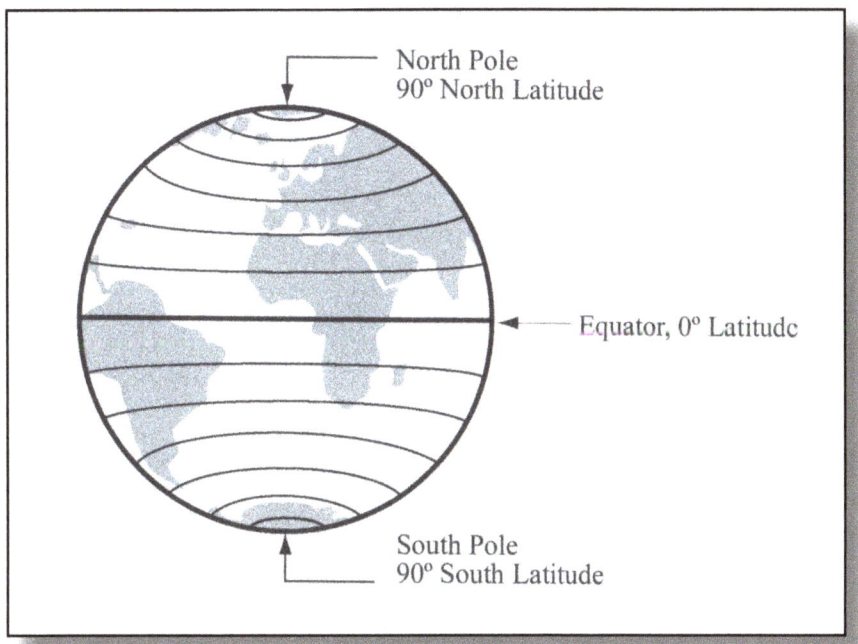

Figure 1. Latitude

Lines of *latitude* that are north of the equator have a "North" designation. *Latitude* lines that are south of the equator have a "South" designation. The *latitude* at the equator is "zero degree." The *latitude* at the North Pole is ninety degrees North. At the South Pole the *latitude* is ninety degrees South.

Longitude is a series of imaginary lines that circle the planet and define positions in the east and west directions on the Earth's surface. These lines are great circle lines whose circumferences pass through the North and South Poles—that is, the center of each great circle, or meridian, is the center of the Earth.

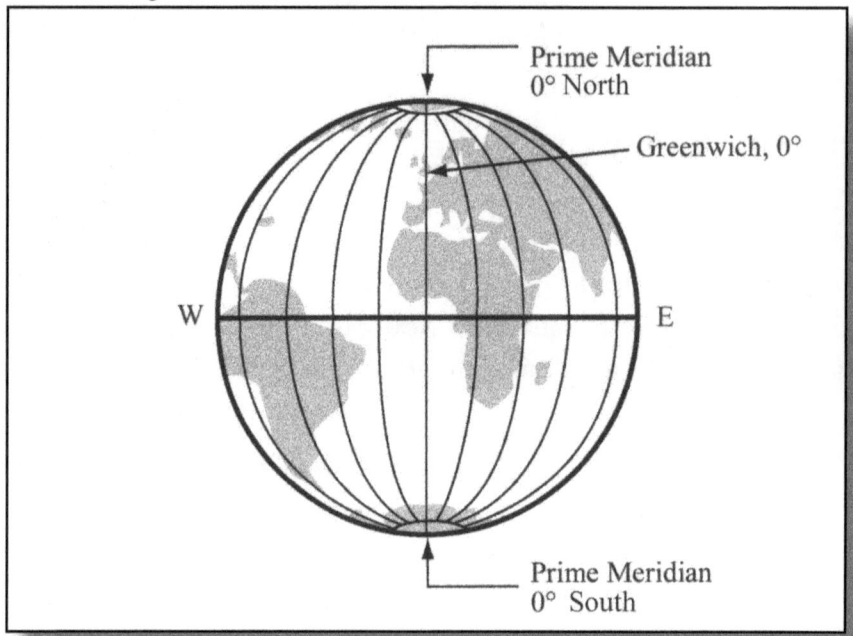

Figure 2a. Longitude at the Prime Meridian

The *prime meridian* is zero degrees *longitude*, and it describes the circumference of a great circle that passes through the Royal Observatory at Greenwich, England. One hundred eighty (180) degrees *longitude* is in the Pacific Ocean, exactly opposite of Greenwich, and it is the International Date Line. Meridians to the east of Greenwich have an East designation; those to the west have a West designation.

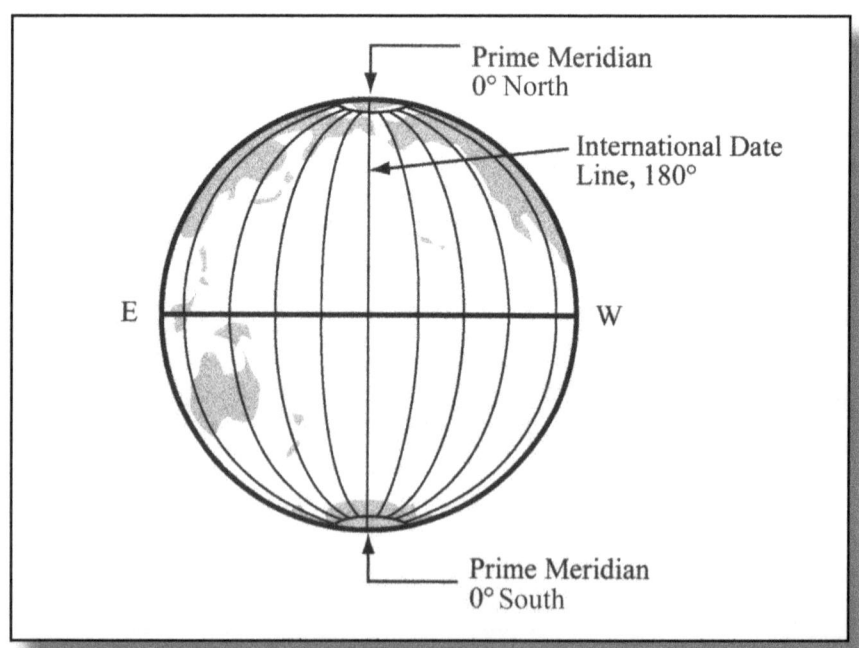

Figure 2b. Longitude at the International Date Line

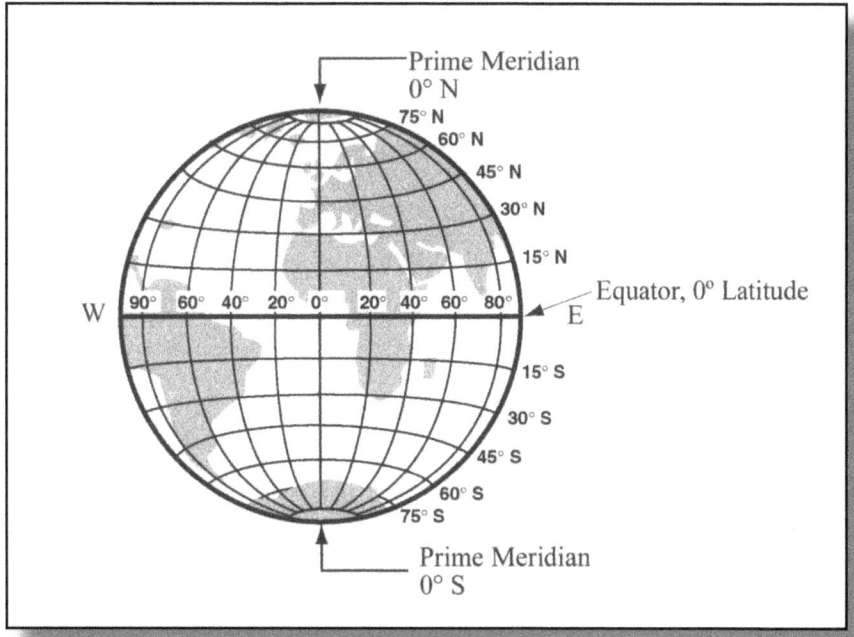

Figure 2c. Latitudes and Longitudes in Western Hemisphere

Degrees of *latitude* and *longitude* are divided into minutes and seconds.

One degree = 60 minutes

One minute = 60 seconds

Assuming that the Earth is a perfect sphere (which it is not, but it's very close), we define a nautical mile as one minute of *longitude*, or one degree of *latitude* at the equator. Thus, one nautical mile is approximately 6,080 feet.

For instance, the location of the Belmont Mill historic site in White Pine County, Nevada, is

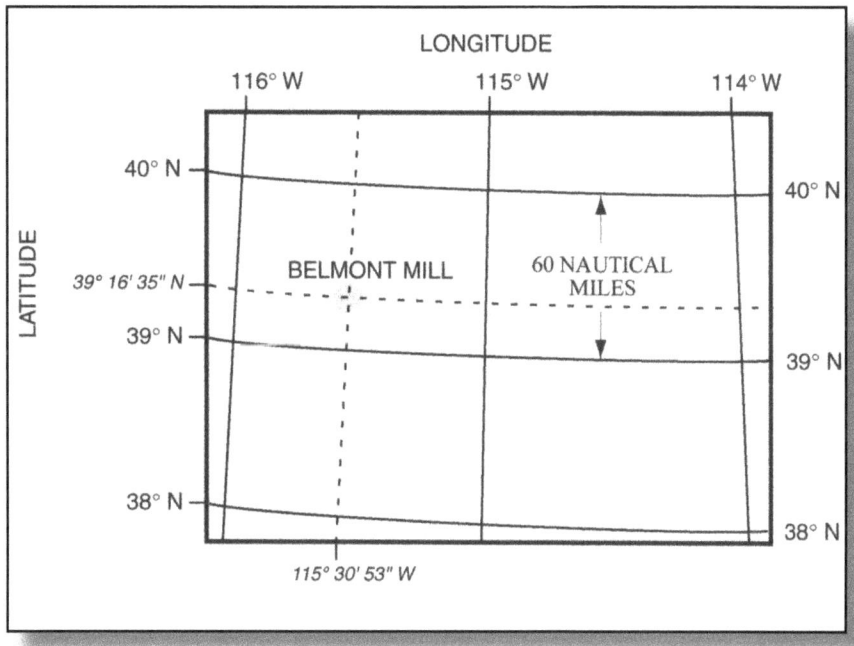

Figure 3. Locating Belmont Mill, Nevada Using Latitude and Longitude

- Latitude: 39 degrees, 16 minutes, and 35 seconds, North.
- Longitude: 115 degrees, 30 minutes, and 53 seconds, West.

Restating this location in standard symbols: 39° 16' 35" N/115° 30' 53" W.

Using the above *latitude* and *longitude* (lat. and long. or simply L/L.), we know the location of Belmont Mill to within 101 feet. Let's see how this works.

      1 degree (°) latitude = 60 nautical miles = 364,800 feet.

      1 minute (') latitude = one nautical mile = 6,080 feet.

      1 second (") latitude = 101 feet.

I determine the latitude and longitude of the sites by using:

- GPS readings at the site.
- And, when possible, by measurements on the 1:24K USGS topographic maps.*

Many GPS instruments give minutes of latitude and longitude in decimal form. For instance, a reading might be 37° 50.78N/117° 34.87W. To change the minutes expressed in decimals to seconds, multiply the decimal number by 60.

      Thus, our example reads: 37° 50' 46.8"N/117° 34' 52.2".

*The symbol colon (:) is used to indicate a proportion or ratio. For example, 1:24K means that one (1) measure on a map equal 24,000 measures on the ground. At this ratio, or scale, individual houses are spotted on topographic maps. The measure could be in any dimension: inches, centimeters, feet, miles, kilometers, furlongs, etc.

Chemung Mine, CA
Date of Photograph: 14 April, 1997
Ghost Town Rating: 8
Road Condition Rating: 3

Abandoned Machinery, Hamilton, NV
Date of Photograph: 23 October, 1994
Ghost Town Rating: 8
Road Condition Rating: 3

Valedon, NM
Date of Photograph: 27 October 2002
Ghost Town Rating: 7
Road Condition Rating: 2

Pontotoc, TX
Date of Photograph: 31 July, 2011
Ghost Town Rating: 4
Road Condition Rating: 1

Grantsville, NV
Date of Photograph: 17 November, 1989
Ghost Town Rating: 7
Road Condition Rating: 2

Penwell, TX
Date of Photograph: 7 November, 2005
Ghost Town Rating: 5
Road Condition Rating: 1

James Stuart House, Bodie, CA
Date of Photograph: 7 November, 2005
Ghost Town Rating: 10
Road Condition Rating: 2

Sasco, AZ
Date of Photograph: 18 November, 2006
Ghost Town Rating: 5
Road Condition Rating: 3

Chapter Six

Driving Tips

Ghost towning is serious business, and **safety** must be our foremost consideration while exploring in the backcountry. Detailed planning, common sense, intimate knowledge, and prudent caution are the prime requirements for a ghost town trip. Most of the sites are located in mountainous areas where roads frequently are rough, deeply rutted, washed out, sandy, and with large rocks buried in the roadbed. Four-wheel drive vehicles with high clearance are imperative for serious ghost town exploration.

Here are some tips that I've found helpful over the many years I've been ghost towning. This list is not all-inclusive, so I urge you to do your own research to supplement these suggestions with your own.

My most important tip is to take water, water, and more water. Other than your vehicle, water is your most important asset. The warmer the climate, the more water a person requires. There's more about water in Chapter Eleven.

The next most important tip is to tell a responsible person where you're going. Are you camping and for how long? What is your return date and the approximate time? If you don't check in with them within a reasonable time after your scheduled return, they'll notify the authorities—usually the county sheriff. Critically important: When you do return on schedule, make sure that you notify the "responsible person" so that they do not raise a false alarm.

A sturdy four-wheel-drive vehicle is essential for any travel off the main roads. It's better if the vehicle has a winch with steel cable and hook. Ideally, it's best to travel in a two-vehicle caravan. Back road/trail travel usually is slow, rough, hard on the passengers, and even harder on the vehicle.

- Ensure that your vehicle is in top-notch mechanical condition.
- Before each sojourn into the backcountry, check all fluid levels, hoses, fan belts, and tires (including the spare), and top off the gasoline tank.
- Check the ground underneath the vehicle for signs of fluid loss.
- Carry spare oil, radiator fluid, gasoline, power steering and brake fluids, fan belts, and a hand-operated tire pump.
- Carry appropriate tools to make minor repairs.
- Check the weather forecast. Don't get caught in a snowstorm or a flash flood.
- Carry a mountain bicycle or an all-terrain vehicle, if possible.
- Carry a snatch-block pulley with steel cable and hook. The pulley doubles the power of the winch.

Today, many vehicles are automatic four-wheel drive. Nonetheless, I don't trust them. I'm an ol' fashion type fellow. I prefer a vehicle with the manual four-wheel system. Any time I drive on backcountry roads or trails, I keep my vehicle in four-wheel-drive, high setting. Such precautionary practice increases traction, helps keep the wheels straight, controls the wheels in sharp turns, and keeps the vehicle moving in unexpected, minor road hazards. Maintaining momentum is essential. I use low setting only when driving in deep sand or in very rough terrain. Sooner or later, however, your vehicle will get stuck.

There are two kinds of "stuck"—high centered and bogged down in soft sand, loose gravel or rocks, and mud. Sometimes one gets stuck both ways. When the vehicle is high centered, some or all of the wheels are off the ground and cannot generate traction. High centering is caused by driving the vehicle over a rock or outcropping that the axle or other parts of the undercarriage do not clear. Winch out if you can, or have the other vehicle in your caravan pull you out. If those options are not viable, try to dig out the offending obstacle. If that's not possible, jack up a set of wheels, raising the axle above the rock. Pack rocks and other stuff under the raised wheels—enough to generate some traction. Drive off slowly.

If you are bogged down in sand, mud, or gravel, don't spin the wheels. You'll only dig yourself in deeper. Determine which direction, forward or backward, is the best way to go. If that's not feasible, jack up a set of wheels. Put rocks, brush, anything that'll generate traction under the upraised wheel. Deflate the tires to about 10 pounds pressure to give the vehicle more traction. With the vehicle in four-wheel, low-drive setting, ease out with tender pressure on the accelerator. It might be necessary to rock the vehicle forward and backward until you get onto firmer ground. Be sure to inflate the tires to proper pressure with the hand pump before proceeding.

Sometimes when traveling in the backcountry, the road or trail becomes steep. In addition to uphill/downhill, I mean from side to side. This condition is found oftentimes on mountain trails. Be careful. Your vehicle is apt to tilt and roll over, which is, perhaps, the ultimate backcountry driving tragedy. Depending on the circumstance, it might be prudent to stop and hike to the site. Consider the risk/reward scenario.

- How close is the site?
- Is the site worth the effort (assuming you have done your preplanning)?
- What are the weather conditions?
- What is your strength, endurance, and general health?
- You fill in the rest of this list with your perspective.

Sometimes you are tempted to drive off-road: it's a shortcut, the road down the hill looks to be better, etc. I don't endorse off-road driving. It's dangerous. But if circumstances *demand* it, caution is forefront. If the slope is not excessive, always go straight up or down, or as close to it as possible. Do not cross a hill at an angle; you'll be gambling on a rollover.

One last thought. Carl Austin says in his book *Common Sense in Desert Travel,* "(Your) wheels can take you farther in minutes than you can hike back from in hours or even days."

Bodie School, CA
Date of Photograph: 1 August 1981
Ghost Town Rating: 10
Road Condition Rating: 2

Pueblo, TX
Date of Photograph: 14 April, 2012
Ghost Town Rating: 8
Road Condition Rating: 3

Barstow, TX
Date of Photograph: 15 April, 2012
Ghost Town Rating: 7
Road Condition Rating: 1

Ruby, AZ
Date of Photograph: 5 November, 2005
Ghost Town Rating: 9
Road Condition Rating: 2

Ballarat, CA
Date of Photograph: 28 October, 1997
Ghost Town Rating: 6
Road Condition Rating: 2

Winter Ranch, NV
Date of Photograph: 24 October, 2000
Ghost Town Rating: 4
Road Condition Rating: 4

Jerome, AZ
Date of Photograph: 5 November, 1993
Ghost Town Rating: 8
Road Condition Rating: 1

Schoolhouse, Kent, TX
Date of Photograph: 17, October 2007
Ghost Town Rating: 3
Road Condition Rating: 1

CHAPTER SEVEN

ROAD CONDITION RATING SYSTEM

A primary concern when ghost towning in the backcountry is the condition of the roads/trails leading to the sites. To aid the ghost towers in planning trips, I developed a road condition ratings system that ranges from "1" to "5". "1" is the best, and "5" the worst (details below). I based my assessment of road conditions as they were on the day that I visited the site. Be assured that over time, these conditions will change—and generally they'll change for the worse.

I rated the road conditions based on the worst-case scenario. That is, what's the worst road condition encountered en route to the historic site. For instance, if I traveled extensively on a paved road and several good gravel roads, but for a only a few hundred yards on a trail on which a four-wheel-drive vehicle was needed, then the site road condition rating is tabbed a "5"—"four-wheel-drive vehicle is necessary."

Road Condition Ratings
1. Highway or paved road.
2. Excellent gravel or dirt road, well maintained.
3. Rough gravel or dirt road, with ruts, holes, extensive washboards, and steep inclines. Four-wheel drive is prudent.
4. Road or trail in deteriorated condition, narrow mountain road, sharp inclines, deep ruts, and deep sand. Four-wheel drive recommended.
5. Same as condition "4," plus: trail is extremely rough, very steep inclines or twisting, narrow trail, rocks in the road, or road washouts. Four-wheel drive required.

I strongly urge the ghost towner not to venture off main roads without a four-wheel-drive vehicle and to have the knowledge of how to use it skillfully. Sometimes, I found that because I had a four-wheel-drive vehicle, my partner and I would venture onto a site that we would otherwise have skipped. Sometimes, we'd find that the road was good enough that a four-wheel-drive vehicle was not necessary or was required minimally for short stretches. Here's the important point—because we were in a four-wheel-drive vehicle, we had confidence in our ability to get to the historic site and return. We took no (or only minimal) chances on getting stuck or high-centered somewhere in the outback. If things got too rough, we'd get out of our vehicle and hike to the site.

For example, in our trek to Silver Dyke, Nevada, the steep mountain trail was littered with rocks. Several times, I exited the vehicle and cleared the trail. No matter, the road condition became near impassable and dangerous. We left our four-wheeler carrying our weapons, water, and cameras and hiked the remaining thousand yards to this outstanding site.

Old Hichita South, NM
Date of Photograph: 28 October, 2002
Ghost Town Rating: 7
Road Condition Rating: 4

Silver Dyke, NV
Date of Photograph: 16 April, 1997
Ghost Town Rating: 8
Road Condition Rating: 5

Old Iron Town, UT
Date of Photograph: 26 September, 1992
Ghost Town Rating: 3
Road Condition Rating: 3

Japanese-American Internment Camp, Manzanar, CA
Date of Photograph: 1 April, 1982
Ghost Town Rating: 3
Road Condition Rating: 2

Pecos, TX
Date of Photograph: 15 April, 2012
Ghost Town Rating: 6
Road Condition Rating: 1

Sasco, AZ
Date of Photograph: 18 November, 2006
Ghost Town Rating: 5
Road Condition Rating: 3

Hillsboro, NM
Date of Photograph: 24 October, 2007
Ghost Town Rating: 3
Road Condition Rating: 1

Burbank, UT
Date of Photograph: 1 November, 1998
Ghost Town Rating: 5
Road Condition Rating: 2

Chapter Eight

Cautions

Ghost towning is serious business, but with rational prudence, it can be lots of fun. Nonetheless, there are many ways to get into serious trouble quickly and unknowingly. We need to plan our trip carefully and to prepare for contingencies. In this chapter, I'll discuss some physical dangers and diseases endemic to the Western states. In later chapters, I'll review inclement weather, automobile trouble, cantankerous animals, medical emergencies, and just plain craziness.

We need be aware of many physical dangers as we traipse around the sites. I can't detail all of them. Common sense ought to prevail. Here are some that are peculiar to the West.

Toxic chemicals
Most ghost towns were associated with mining, which used lots of noxious chemicals to process the ore. It's not uncommon for such sites to be contaminated with such chemicals as:

- Mercury
- Lead
- Cyanide compounds
- All manner of hazardous waste

Until fairly recently, concerns about the impact of mining on our environment were minimal at best. Oftentimes when a mine played out or a mill closed, no attempt was made to sanitize the area. Folks just walked away. Consequently, hazardous chemicals may be strewn over the area intermixed with the sand and clay, stacked in sheds, or dissolved in settling ponds. For instance, at Hamilton in White Pine County, one of Nevada's largest sites, I found several dozen large containers labeled **"Potassium Cyanide"** stored in the open behind a dilapidated barbed-wire fence. (Potassium cyanide is the deadly chemical that was used in the San Quentin gas chamber.) On a quick inspection, I figured that these containers were unopened. To record this hazard, I photographed these containers. **WARNING:** Never, under any circumstance, handle this sort of material.

Another example: several years ago my partner and I were photographing the ruins of Gila Mine at Reveille in Nye County. In the draw, there were three large settling ponds that had a greenish-yellow "goop" in them. Just looking at this stuff from atop the hill and speculating what deadly chemicals were in them was enough of a "red light" for us to keep far away. Nearby, my partner found a seriously rusted sign buried in the sand that said "DANGER CYANIDE." Should you find such hazards, please notify the authorities.

Open mine pits

Mine pits abound, and sometimes they are covered with sagebrush and are difficult to see. Some pits are narrow and deep. Falling into one most certainly will cause you severe physical damage. Most pits are impossible to climb out—especially if you're seriously hurt. Unless your partner has the proper equipment and training, you're probably going to stay there until professional help arrives—provided, of course, that you have a partner. If not…

Current law requires that abandoned mine pits be fenced with barbed wire and clearly marked with danger signs. However, many older and abandoned mines do not have such warnings. Be extra cautious when scouting such sites.

Several years ago my partner and I were photographing the Lodi site (AKA Illinois) in Northwestern Nye County, Nevada. We were driving to the head frame, up a steep, narrow trail. I glanced out the passenger window and much to my horror saw that our front wheel was just inches from a gaping mine pit. My driver could not see the pit because it was covered with sagebrush. Fortunately, we missed it. However, had our wheel hit this hole or the ground collapsed at the pit's edge, our vehicle would have slipped in and no telling what the outcome would have been. I can assure you that we were extra careful backing down this road—there was no turnaround at the head frame.

Mine Openings and Adits

Many mines are cut into the side of a hill or mountain, and some entrances are accessible easily. It is seriously unwise to enter a mine (i.e. stupid). Dangers abound. Floorings are weak and a fall through several layers below is possible. Bracing timbers are rotted and any disturbance might cause them to collapse, causing a cave-in. Some animals you don't want to meet might take umbrage at your intrusion into their home. Also, there's the danger of contracting valley fever (see below). **Don't enter mines. No exceptions!**

Explosives

Dynamite and blasting caps were used extensively in mining operations. Unfortunately, at some abandoned mines some of these explosives were left in place. Explosives pose a super serious danger. **WARNING.** Never in any circumstance handle, shoot at, or otherwise disturb explosives. If you spot such items, leave them alone and report your finding to the local authorities.

I have some experience in handling explosives. As explosives age, they become unstable—the older they are, the more unstable. I've seen dynamite sticks "sweat": the nitroglycerin oozes through to the outside of the container and forms into small beads. BAD stuff. Absolutely, leave them alone.

Many years ago, I worked on a geophysical crew. We used specially-made dynamite to make underground explosions so that our equipment could record the reflecting sound waves. On one occasion, I had to cut the sticks into small slices to make mini-charges. I spotted a small sweat bead on one stick and, without much reflection, flicked it off the stick to the ground. I was staggered at the size of the explosion. No damage done except to my composure. Another result of that day's work handling cut-open dynamite was one of the worst headaches I've ever had. The "nitro" was absorbed through my skin and caused a severe toxic reaction.

Unsafe Structures

Many of the structures at the sites are old, rotted, and unstable. Weather, time, and vandals have taken their toll. I suggest that you do not enter structures at the sites. It's dangerous in addition to the peril of HPS (see below). Your weight might be just enough to cause the floor to collapse, leaving you sprawled in the cellar. Any slight disturbance might be just enough to cause the roof to fall in or a wall to collapse. Additionally, there are abandoned and uncovered wells at some of the sites. Always look where you step. A walking stick is appropriate.

Fire

There's always danger of fire in sagebrush country and in the tree-covered mountains during the dry season. Generally, you should have plenty of warning of a fire in the area you plan to visit. Stay out. If you spot a fire in your area, get out and promptly notify the authorities. It's prudent to have an escape plan to the nearest decent road.

Of course, you are a disciple of "Smoky the Bear" and diligently heed his advice about fire precautions. Unknowingly, you can be the culprit who starts a fire in sagebrush country. As you drive over sagebrush, some of it can become entangled in the vehicle undercarriage. Your catalytic converter on the bottom of the vehicle is very hot. Under the right conditions, when dry sagebrush comes in contact with the catalytic converter it can ignite. The resulting fire can destroy your vehicle and start a sagebrush fire. Be aware and take precautions.

To conclude, my message is: Take heed and be aware, circumspect, and cautious about the hazards I've outlined.

Cortez, NV
Date of Photograph: 17 November, 2000
Ghost Town Rating: 6
Road Condition Rating: 2

Fort Churchill, NV
Date of Photograph: 12 April, 1994
Ghost Town Rating: 7
Road Condition Rating: 2

Bodie, CA
Date of Photograph: 1 August, 1981
Ghost Town Rating: 10
Road Condition Rating: 2

Atolia, CA
Date of Photograph: 27 December, 1997
Ghost Town Rating: 8
Road Condition Rating: 1

Cleator, AZ
Date of Photograph: 16 November, 2006
Ghost Town Rating: 7
Road Condition Rating: 2

Elizabethtown, NM
Date of Photograph: 11 October, 2007
Ghost Town Rating: 3
Road Condition Rating: 1

Fire Station, Bodie, CA
Date of Photograph: 1 August, 1981
Ghost Town Rating: 10
Road Condition Rating: 2

Green Street, Bodie, CA
Date of Photograph: 1 August, 1981
Ghost Town Rating: 10
Road Condition Rating: 2

Chapter Nine

Environment-Related Medical Conditions

Weather extremes can cause several medical conditions that we ought to be aware. Below I've listed several of the most common. This list is not complete nor is it comprehensive. Rather, it's an introduction to the topic and I am not a medical professional. I urge you to dig further into the subject so that you'll be better able to recognize symptoms and render first aid.

Heatstroke
A serious threat to life. Excessive exposure to heat causes severe deregulation of the body's thermostat. Sweating stops. Symptoms are excessive body temperature (up to 112 degrees Fahrenheit), hot and dry skin, headache, confusion, convulsions, rapid pulse, unconsciousness, and perhaps coma. Prompt first aid is essential. Cool the patient with cool (not cold) fluids or ice compresses on neck, chest, stomach, and groin. Move the patient to a cool, shady place. Fan to increase evaporation. Get the patient to a medical facility promptly. Without prompt treatment the patient's body systems fail and death results.

Heat exhaustion or heat prostration
Overexposure to heat (usually in combination with other factors, such as drinking alcoholic beverages) causes dehydration and loss of electrolytes, knocking the body's electrochemistry askew. Heat exhaustion is more common in humid climes, which prevent the sweat from evaporating, resulting in a loss of cooling. Symptoms are profuse sweating; pale, clammy skin; weak and rapid pulse; low blood pressure; severe headache; nausea; dizziness; blurred vision and perhaps heat cramps; and occasionally unconsciousness. First aid is to cool the patient. Administer water and salts (sodium and potassium); use salt tablets or table salt for sodium and bananas or other fruit for potassium. Get the patient to a medical facility promptly.

Sunburn
Overexposure of the skin to ultraviolet rays of the sun (or other sources) causes inflammation of the skin. Symptoms are redness, swelling, pain, and blisters. Can be severe, resulting in second-degree burns. First aid is to cover the skin with light clothing, apply cool compresses, and administer appropriate burn medication.

Frostbite or chilblain
Extreme overexposure to cold causes freezing of body parts. Extremities are usually affected first—fingers, hands, feet, ears, and nose. Symptoms are hard white areas on the affected part, with numbness, pale and glossy skin, and maybe blistering. Severe frostbite may require amputation. Get the patient into a warm environment. Bathe affected body part in warm water. Don't massage. Get the patient to a medical facility as soon as possible.

Hypothermia

Extended exposure to cold causes a drop in **body temperature**. Hypothermia has three classifications:

- Mild. 95 degrees to 90 degrees Fahrenheit.
- Moderate. 90 to 86 degrees.
- Life-threatening severe hypothermia. 86 degrees or lower.

Symptoms ranging from mild to severe are shivering, increased blood pressure and respiratory rate, cool to cold legs and arms, pale skin, difficulty speaking, confusion, and stupor. With severe hypothermia, the patient is comatose with dilated pupils that don't respond to light, respiration is slow and shallow or missing, blood pressure is low or zero, and pulse rate is slow or nonexistent.

Treatment varies considerably with the degree of hypothermia the patient experiences. In the most severe cases, where there is no pulse, start cardiopulmonary resuscitation (CPR). And get the victim as quickly as possible to professional medical help. In all cases, warm the patient from one to two degrees per hour. Use blankets, warm and dry clothes, warm liquids; place patient in a warm environment (inside the vehicle with the heater turned on), lie next to the patient under the blanket.

All the medical conditions mentioned here require expert medical attention. Consult the Centers for Disease Control for details.

- CDC URL, www.cdc.gov/contact/index.htm*
- CDC general telephone number, 1-800-232-4636*

* current as of 7 May, 2016

Harquahala, AZ
Date of Photograph: 12 November 2006
Ghost Town Rating: 4
Road Condition Rating: 2

L → R, Morgue, Odd Fellows Lodge, Miner's Union Hall, Bodie, CA
Date of Photograph: 1 August, 1981
Ghost Town Rating: 10
Road Condition Rating: 2

Giddings, TX
Date of Photograph: 9 April, 2006
Ghost Town Rating: 5
Road Condition Rating: 1

Cloverdale, NV
Date of Photograph: 12 April, 1999
Ghost Town Rating: 7
Road Condition Rating: 2

Mariscal Mercury Mine , TX
Date of Photograph: 12 July, 2013
Ghost Town Rating: 7
Road Condition Rating: 3

Kentucky Camp, AZ
Date of Photograph: 7 November, 2007
Ghost Town Rating: 5
Road Condition Rating: 2

Hagan, NM
Date of Photograph: 24 October, 2007
Ghost Town Rating: 3
Road Condition Rating: 2

Belmont Mill, NV
Date of Photograph: 24 October, 1993
Ghost Town Rating: 7
Road Condition Rating: 4

Chapter Ten

Endemic Diseases

As we traipse about the Western states in our ghost towning activities, let's be aware that certain diseases are endemic in this area. In this chapter, I'll discuss four diseases that are of singular interest to us. They are:

- Hantavirus Pulmonary Syndrome (HPS)
- Valley Fever (*coccidioidomycosis*)
- Bubonic Plague
- Giardiasis

Hantavirus Pulmonary Syndrome (HPS)

HPS is a serious viral infection of the lung. The mortality rate is about 45 percent. Breathing dust contaminated by infected mice is the primary source of this virus. Deer mice are the principal carrier of hantavirus. Other rodents also may be carriers, for example, the cotton rat, white-footed mouse, and other unidentified species.

Infected rodents spread the virus in their urine, droppings, saliva, and nesting materials. If we were to stir this material, tiny droplets containing the virus would get airborne and contaminate the air we breathe. We also can get the virus by eating contaminated food, or by touching contaminated material and then touching our nose or mouth. In rare cases, the virus is transmitted by a rodent bite.

The symptoms of Hantavirus appear in one to six weeks after exposure. The initial symptoms are severe muscle aches, chills, and fever. Oftentimes abdominal pain, vomiting, and nausea follow. In a week or so, some patients will have shortness of breath and coughing. Serious breathing difficulties usually follow.

Here are a few precautions you can take to minimize exposure to Hantavirus:

- Pay attention to posted signs. For example, at Mount Hope in Eureka County signs are posted on many of the buildings that read "DANGER: DO NOT ENTER. POTENTIAL EXPOSURE TO HANTAVIRUS"
- Avoid areas with rodent droppings.
- Don't disturb rodent nests.
- Do not enter cabins, sheds, etc., which are ideal places for nests and dens.
- Do not sleep on the ground. Use a blanket, etc.
- Keep food in tightly covered containers.
- Wash dishes and utensils immediately after using them. Not in streams, however. More on this topic below under "Giardiasis."

I just touched on the highlights of this disease. I suggest that you do further research.

I gleaned the material I've discussed in this section from two web sites.

1. The Public Health of Seattle and King County

http://www.kingcounty.gov/healthservices/health/communicable/diseases/hantavirus.aspx

    2. The Centers for Disease Control

        http://www.cdc.gov/ncidod/diseases/hanta/hps/noframes/at_risk.htm

Valley Fever

Valley fever is a lung disease caused by breathing the spores of the fungus *Coccidoides immitis.* This fungus grows in the ground where precipitation is minimal, summers are warm, and winters are mild—our Western states. The fungus spores become airborne when wind, construction, vehicle traffic, or our trampling disturbs the ground. In most cases, our body's defense mechanism resolves this disease without any treatment. In fact, most folks who live in infected areas eventually test positive for the disease even though they did not experience severe symptoms—usually accepted as a mild case of influenza. However, sometimes Valley Fever can be serious and requires hospitalization. People who have an increased risk are those with immune system deficiencies, HIV, organ transplants, diabetes, third trimester pregnancy, or Hodgkin's disease.

    If a person is infected with a high concentration of spores, it's likely that the infection will be severe. **Important:** large concentrations of the fungal spores are often found in abandoned buildings, cabins, mines, burial grounds, and rodent nests. In fact, the entrance areas of most mines are contaminated with these spores—some intensely so. Here's yet another valid reason not to enter abandoned mines.

    Symptoms generally occur three weeks after exposure and include fatigue, cough, chest pain, fever, rash, headache, and joint aches. In severe cases, the patient may get fungal pneumonia, skin lesions, or infected bones and joints. Meningitis is the most serious and possibly lethal complication of the disease. Treatment consists of various antifungal drug therapies. In severe cases, evidence of the disease may linger for years and require hospitalization.

    I've synopsized this information on Valley Fever from two web sites:

    1. The Valley Fever Center for Excellence, Tucson, Arizona

        http://vfce.arizona.edu/

    2. The Mayo Clinic

        http://www.mayoclinic.org/diseases-conditions/valley-fever/basics/definition/con-20027390

Bubonic Plague

It's an ancient, highly contagious disease: the Black Death, which scourged Europe in the 14th century—decimating about 50 percent of the population (about 200 million people). During the westward migration in the USA, bubonic plague was a serious threat. Though not as serious a threat nowadays as it was in the past, bubonic plague is of some concern for us in the West. Ten to fifteen cases of this disease are diagnosed each year in the USA.

    Bubonic plague is caused by the bacillus bacterium, *Yersina pestis.* The vector for this bacterium is the rat flea (*Xenopsylla cheopsi*s). A bite by an infected flea is the source of the infection. The hosts for such fleas are rodents. In the West, the rock squirrel and the ground squirrel are the most common hosts. Other rodents that serve as hosts are prairie dogs, chipmunks, wood rats, wild mice, voles, and other rodent species.

    Symptoms begin within two to six days after exposure, and they include swollen, extremely painful lymph nodes, headache, chills, and extreme malaise. Should this disease not be treated, the bacterium spreads to the blood causing abdominal pain, shock, and bleeding into the skin, which subsequently turns black. (Hence its nickname "Black Death.") If not treated, the fatality rate is about 75 percent. Early diagnosis is critical. Antibiotics are highly effective in controlling this disease if given early.

    I've synopsized this information about bubonic plague from two web sites.

    1. The Entomology Department, Virginia Tech

        https://www.researchcompliance.vt.edu/iacuc/training/faqs/plague

2. The Association of State and Territorial Directors of Health Promotion and Public Health Education

http://www.astdhpphe.org/infect/plague.html

Giardiasis (beaver fever)

Giardia infection (giardiasis) is an intestinal infection caused by a microscopic parasite *(Giardia lamblia)* that's found in streams and lakes. The usual contamination results from animal feces and urine in the water. Many deer in the West have this parasite. Symptoms appear in one or two weeks after exposure and they include abdominal cramps, bloating, nausea, fatigue, weight loss, and bouts of watery diarrhea—resulting in dehydration. Treatment is specific antibiotics.

On a trip in Washoe County, several years ago, I washed my hunting knife in a fast-running stream. Dumb! Later I used this knife to cut an apple. Guess what? A few days later, I was seriously sick with Giardia. In the Emergency Room at Renown Hospital in Reno, the doctor prescribed two liters of saline solution and an antibiotic with the proviso that I not drink anything with alcohol or use alcohol on my skin. Released, I recovered fully in two days.

For more information about Giardia please consult:

1. Centers for Disease Control and Prevention

https://www.cdc.gov/parasites/giardia/

2. Mayo Clinic

http://www.mayoclinic.org/diseases-conditions/giardia-infection/basics/definition/con-20024686

Conclusion

If you experience any of the symptoms described in this chapter after a trip to the wilds of the West, promptly seek medical attention. Tell the physician where you've been and what you suspect is the source of your illness.

I included this chapter to make you aware of some diseases that can possibly cause you trouble, however remote. My goal is not to scare you away but to give you a "heads up"—to heighten your awareness of some of the risks of ghost towning so that you can take precautions.

With appropriate safeguards, it's highly unlikely that you'd contract any of the diseases discussed here. You can have a fine time exploring the backcountry, finding ghost towns, and getting those outstanding photographs.

Bell, NM
Date of Photograph: 12 October, 2007
Ghost Town Rating: 4
Road Condition Rating: 1

Harrisburg, UT
Date of Photograph: 28 September, 1992
Ghost Town Rating: 5
Road Condition Rating: 2

Calera Chapel, Toyahvalle, TX
Date of Photograph: 14 November, 2005
Ghost Town Rating: 4
Road Condition Rating: 2

Colfax, NM
Date of Photograph: 11 October, 2007
Ghost Town Rating: 4
Road Condition Rating: 2

Charcoal Ovens, Mahogany Flat, CA
Date of Photograph: 8 December, 1990
Ghost Town Rating: 5
Road Condition Rating: 2

General Store, Pearce, AZ
Date of Photograph: 4 November, 2005
Ghost Town Rating: 5
Road Condition Rating: 1

Winston, NM
Date of Photograph: 23 October, 2002
Ghost Town Rating: 4
Road Condition Rating: 1

Yeso, NM
Date of Photograph: 9 Octover, 2007
Ghost Town Rating: 5
Road Condition Rating: 2

Chapter Eleven

Water

Water is a lifesaver. In summertime, water (pure, clean, potable water) is your most important asset. It's **CRITICALLY IMPORTANT** to prevent dehydration. Conservation and replenishment of body fluids is paramount. On average in midsummer, with moderate activity, the literature posits that a person needs about three quarts to a gallon per day.

Additionally, your body needs the electrolytes sodium and potassium to regulate the fluid levels, manage blood pressure, and keep the body's cells in balance. Sources for electrolytes are salt tablets, bananas, other fruits, and sports drinks.

Here are some facts: in midsummer with the air temperature in the 100-degree range and without shade, you can survive for about two days without water. After two days, you become seriously dehydrated and experience rapid body and mental fatigue—resulting in unconsciousness. Death occurs in three to four days.

Should you get into a survival situation, drink only water! From time to time refresh your body with sport drinks. Drinking anything else results in a net loss of body fluids because it takes more water for the body to process the food materials contained in these fluids than the drinks contain. Such food materials are milk, colas (non-diet), etc. Under no condition, drink urine, radiator fluid, or alcoholic beverages. Instead, consider pouring these liquids on your body and especially your head to cool it. However, be prepared to tolerate flies and other insects. Nonetheless, keeping your body as cool as possible is essential.

There's water to be found. Scattered throughout the desert and mountain areas of the West are springs, streams, creeks, wells, and pools. Many mountain gullies, ravines, and draws have a stream—however short and meager. Oftentimes, such water sources are shown on 1:24K topographic maps. Most of these water sources are fresh water and are potable <u>after treatment</u>.

Caution: Most of the water in the "wild" probably is contaminated with parasites, heavy metals, and other noxious stuff. (See Chapter Ten for details.) Use water-purification tablets to kill bacteria before drinking such water. These tablets usually are an iodine compound.

Filtering water through charcoal filters reduces significantly heavy metals and other noxious stuff. Sporting goods, Army surplus, and other types of stores stock charcoal filter kits and water purification tablets.

Only drink untreated stream water in an emergency. Of course, if your situation is desperate and you're out of tablets and charcoal filters, drink. It's better to take a chance on getting sick than dehydrating.

Be cautious with pooled or standing water. It is probably contaminated and may well be "salt" water. **DON'T EVER DRINK SALT WATER.** <u>No exceptions</u>. Use salt water to cool the body. Desalination is the only way to make salt water potable.

Other sources of water. Water is usually found where there's vegetation, where birds flock at eventide, or where animals gather. Dig in the low point of a bend in a dry creek bed or wash. **CAUTION.** Don't expend an excessive amount of energy (body fluid) digging in a futile effort. If there is water, it ought to be within two or three feet. Cactus pulp has a meager amount of water. Other water-generating techniques are more complicated, and are outside our scope—for example, ground solar stills.

In summary: It's water, water, and water. Carry several gallons for each person in the party.

Bodie, CA
Date of Photograph: 1 August, 1981
Ghost Town Rating: 10
Road Condition Rating: 2

Ibex Spring, CA
Date of Photograph: 22 October, 2001
Ghost Town Rating: 6
Road Condition Rating: 5

Courthouse, Toyah, TX
Date of Photograph: 15 April, 2012
Ghost Town Rating: 4
Road Condition Rating: 2

Hotel, Terlingua, TX
Date of Photograph: 30 July, 2010
Ghost Town Rating: 7
Road Condition Rating: 1

Garlock, CA
Date of Photograph: 9 January, 1996
Ghost Town Rating: 5
Road Condition Rating: 1

Old Nye County Courthouse, Belmont, NV
Date of Photograph: 15 November, 1994
Ghost Town Rating: 8
Road Condition Rating: 3

Villa de la Mina, TX
Date of Photograph: 12 July, 2013
Ghost Town Rating: 9
Road Condition Rating: 2

Movie Set, Dolomite, CA
Date of Photograph: 1 April, 1982
Ghost Town Rating: 7
Road Condition Rating: 2

Chapter Twelve

Survival Kit

Before leaving on a ghost town trip, it's imperative that you prepare a survival kit. In the following list, I've detailed the items that I carried on my trips. Revise it to suit your needs for the place, time of year, and the conditions of the area you'll visit.

I did not list my survival kit items in any particular order. Nor do I claim that the list is complete. Nonetheless, all the items I listed are important. To complete this kit, add items of a personal nature; for example, prescription drugs, glasses, and other items you deem necessary.

Here's my list.

- Two sets of keys for the automobile given to others in your party
- Spare batteries for all battery-powered equipment. Install new batteries for each trip.
- Shoulder pack in which to carry stuff
- Large and strong plastic storage bag
- Survival bag, 3-mil polyethylene, 84- by 36-inch recommended
- Lightweight sleeping bag: one for each person
- Tarpaulin (heavy-gauge plastic tarp) 8- by 8-foot (make lean-to)
- Tent pegs
- Web belt
- Leather gloves
- Reflective (motorcycle type) vest/shirt
- Sunglasses in a case
- Extra pair of your prescription glasses
- Lip balm
- Toilet tissue
- Paper towels
- Towelettes
- Can openers (beer-can and roll types)
- Fire starter system (flint and steel)
- Packet of waterproof matches; one packet for each person
- Small, portable watertight case for matches
- Butane lighter
- Portable canteen, one-quart capacity, in pouch with web belt
- Large water jug, five-gallon capacity, filled

- Heavy-duty plastic one-gallon water-filled jug, at least one per person
- Water treatment and neutralizer tablets
- Dry rations, such as Meal Ready to Eat (MRE), several per person (See Chapter Eleven.)
- Engineer compass
- Whistle
- Signal mirror
- Pedometer
- Hatchet (in case to attach to web belt)
- Large, multipurpose hunting knife, in case, to attach to web belt
- Fencing tool
- Tool kit (screwdrivers, wrenches, hammer, etc.)
- Mylar cord, 1/4 inch thick minimum, 50 foot minimum
- Fish hooks and nylon line
- Fire extinguisher
- Large first-aid kit, with a pair of splints
- Roll of duct tape
- Revolver, 38 caliber or larger
- 100 rounds of ammunition for the gun
- Portable, automobile-compatible cellular/satellite telephone. Portable AM/FM radio, with two sets of spare batteries. My radio had batteries and a hand crank for generating power if all batteries were exhausted.
- Battery-powered waterproof watch
- Car Lite (plugs into auto's cigarette lighter)
- High-power, battery-powered lantern with 6-volt battery
- Long-burning candles
- Trenching shovel (folding handle is okay)
- Six railroad-type signal flares
- Tire chains
- Tire pump (hand type)
- Rain gear
- Cold-weather gear
- Portable Citizen's Band (CB) radio, w/two sets of spare batteries. Know channels of the following:
  - Highway Patrol
  - Local Sheriff
  - Truckers' channels used in your area (available on the Web)

The emergency channel is NINE (9). **Use channel 9 only in an emergency.**
Say, **"MAY DAY, MAY DAY, MAY DAY,"** pause 60 seconds to wait for reply. Repeat MAY DAY message, pause 60 seconds, etc. Continue MAY DAY transmissions for 10 minutes. Then halt. Wait 30 minutes then repeat MAY DAY transmissions. If and when you receive a response, talk clearly and slowly. Give your name. Location. Nature of your emergency. What you expect. If you do not understand an incoming message, respond, "Say again." Wait, and listen carefully for the response. If you are convinced that the sender is trustworthy, do exactly what the incoming message says.

Notes:

- The web belt can be purchased at most sporting or military surplus stores. Ensure that the gear to be attached is compatible with the belt.
- The international distress signal is "SOS." In Morse code, SOS is "dot, dot, dot. dash, dash, dash. dot, dot, dot."
- You can send an international distress signal with your revolver by firing three rounds two seconds apart, much as the "S" in "SOS" in Morse code.
- You can send an SOS with the signal mirror.
- Hand-held iPhones and similar telephones have a limited range in the outback, especially in narrow mountain valleys.

Never, never, send a false message over these Emergency Channels. It's against the law. It will activate rescue parties erroneously. And smacks of the "Cry Wolf" syndrome.

Over the years of ghost towning, I've not been in a dire survival predicament. Nonetheless, I've had a few close calls. Equipment from my survival kit was the key that kept the situation under control.

Ibex Spring, CA
Date of Photograph: 22 October, 2001
Ghost Town Rating: 8
Road Condition Rating: 5

Coyamsa, TX
Date of Photograph: 16 April, 2012
Ghost Town Rating: 5
Road Condition Rating: 2

Barstow, TX
Date of Photograph: 15 April, 2012
Ghost Town Rating: 7
Road Condition Rating: 1

General Store, Tybo, NV
Date of Photograph: 4 September, 1991
Ghost Town Rating: 7
Road Condition Rating: 2

Chemung Mine, CA
Date of Photograph: 14 April, 1997
Ghost Town Rating: 8
Road Condition Rating: 3

Carrara, NV
Date of Photograph: 30 January, 1991
Ghost Town Rating: 6
Road Condition Rating: 3

Copeland, TX
Date of Photograph: 25 February, 2007
Ghost Town Rating: 4
Road Condition Rating: 1

L → R, Odd Fellows Lodge, Miner's Union Hall, Bodie, CA
Date of Photograph: 1 August, 1981
Ghost Town Rating: 10
Road Condition Rating: 2

CHAPTER THIRTEEN

DESERT SURVIVAL

As a former naval intelligence officer trained in survival techniques, I'm opening this chapter with the following maxim:

Of all survival situations, desert survival is the most serious, difficult, and easily gotten into. It can quickly become life threatening. And, unfortunately, oftentimes the person is unaware that he/she is in a life-threatening situation.

In this chapter, I'll discuss only some of the basics of desert survival. I urge you to seek more comprehensive instruction and training.

Climate

IMPORTANT. Each day, before starting ghost towning, check the short-term and long-term weather forecast—make plans accordingly.

Weather is fickle in these climes. It is widely varied and can be extreme—turning from pleasant to wretched in a very short time—no matter the season or environs. I'm no expert on weather. Nonetheless, here are few personal observations:

In the summer, daytime temperatures probably will be intensely hot, bone dry, and windy; evening time can be pleasant to cool.

Winter can be bitterly cold and windy, with a subzero wind-chill; snow and sleet are common, especially in the northern and mountainous environs. Occasionally, heavy snowstorms disrupt travel. On the other hand, the weather can be pleasantly mild. In wintertime, the climate in the southern sections usually is more temperate. However, be prepared for the worst. The weather can turn unseasonable (hot or cold) in just a few hours. And in rainy weather, flash floods are a serious threat.

Spring and autumn are the preferred times for desert travel. I favor autumn because of the colorful foliage and all-day low-sun angle. (Light from a low-sun angle increases contrast and enhances the texture of the subject—such light gives the photograph the three-dimensional look. But, I digress.) Generally, in the spring and autumn, mornings and evenings are chilly and midday is mild. Nonetheless, the weather can be capricious. For instance, in the autumn I've encountered weather that changes from 100 degrees plus to bone-chilling cold in just a day or so.

Dress

How does one dress for such extremes in climate? There are no easy answers. Here's how I do it. I dress in layers, and add and peel as appropriate. Woolens in the cold times. And light-colored, loose-fitting cotton for the warmer times. And combinations in between. I avoid polyester because it does not breathe, and in a fire it melts to your skin. I keep heavy duty, cold-weather gear in our four-wheel-drive vehicle. Included are a rain-proof duster, wool sweater/jacket, wool/leather gloves, long johns, galoshes, and several wool blankets.

No matter the time of year or weather conditions, I always wear long-sleeved shirts buttoned at the cuff, long trousers, white cotton T-shirt and underpants, ankle-high boots, and a high-crowned fedora with a wide brim and eyelets—wool in cool times, and straw for warmer times.

One may wonder why I'm so particular with hats. It's easy. The hat may well be the most important part of my dress. In cool times, we lose an enormous amount of body heat through our heads if not covered. In warm times, the converse is true. The sun pounding on an uncovered head increases body temperature and causes significant loss of body fluids. And conservation of body fluids is essential in desert travel. The crown of a fedora is an air pocket that insulates the head, the brim provides shade, and the eyelets allow circulation.

Varmints, Critters, and Creepy-Crawly Things

Many and varied are the fauna in the Western mountains and deserts: eagles, deer, pronghorn antelope, elk, ducks, geese, mountain lions, and perhaps a bear or two. There are too many to detail here and they are beyond our scope. Instead, I'm going to discuss, in general terms, some insects, reptiles, and mammals of which you ought to be aware.

Other than ants, wasps, and bees, the two critters of special note are the black widow spider and scorpion. The spider bites and the scorpion stings. Both are painful, but they are rarely life threatening. However, they need to be treated. I'm not a medical professional (medico), so my best advice is to get expert medical attention as soon as possible.

NOTE: A few folks are allergic to the venom from these critters and will have a serious reaction. Prompt medical attention is essential.

We find these critters in dark, seldom-disturbed, sheltered rubble and ruins: under rocks, logs, railroad ties, old mining equipment, abandoned shacks, and the like. People usually get bitten and stung by being careless or foolhardy. Avoid the critters and they'll avoid you. Look where you put your hands, sit, and walk.

Reptiles are a different matter. Again, I'm not a medico, nor am I a herpetologist. Thus, my thoughts regarding these reptiles are non-expert. Though there are a number of nonpoisonous snakes in the West, it's the venomous ones with which we have concern.

Leave all snakes alone and they'll leave you alone. They're probably more afraid of you than you are of them. Snakes will not attack unless threatened or disturbed. Fools get bitten when they startle, step on, sit on, or handle them. And rattlesnakes will not always rattle to warn you of an impending strike. Look where you put your hands, feet, and buttocks, especially when stepping out of your automobile or when moving after having been still for an extended period. If, for whatever reason, you need to move or kill a venomous snake, use a long-handled shovel, and cut off the head. And whatever you do, don't touch a "dead" snake. Because of the snake-bite reflex, a dead snake can bite, even a decapitated one. This reflex action can persist for an hour or so. But understand, snakes are an integral part of the desert ecosystem and are best left to themselves.

Below is a list of most of the venomous reptiles in the Western states:

- Copperhead snake (*Agkistroden contortrix*)
- Coral snake (*Micrurus fulvius*—an *Elapidae*)
- Gila monster—lizard (*Geloderma suspecturn*)
- Rattlesnakes
  - Great Basin (*Crotralus viridis*)
  - Massagua (*Sistrurus catenatus*)
  - Mojave Green (*Crotalus scutulatus*)
  - Sidewinder (*Crotalus cerastes*)
  - Southern Pacific (*Crotalus oreganus helleri*)

- Western Diamondback (*Crotalus atrox*)
- Western Pigmy (*Sistrurus miliarius streoken*)
- Timber (*Crotalus horridus*)
- Water moccasin snake, "Cotton Mouth" (*Agkistrodon piscivorus*)

Factors to consider in a venomous bite are, in no particular order:

- Age and health of the one bitten
- Distance (in time) to medical help
- Personnel available to assist the victim; capabilities, qualifications, and mind-set
- Part of the body bitten; farther from the heart and head the better
- The Mojave Green and the Southern Pacific are the most dangerous. They have two types of venom: a neurotoxin that attacks the nervous system and a hemotoxin that attacks the blood and heart.

Swelling and pain are common symptoms from a venomous snakebite. Here are the current first aid procedures:

DO

- Try to keep the patient calm, quiet, and immobile—a tough task, I admit.
- Give water to the patient—and only water.
- Apply a splint to the bitten limb to restrict muscle contraction.
- Remove rings, bracelets, watches, or anything that might restrict blood flow from the bitten limb—the limb will swell.
- Get the patient to medical help as quickly as possible

DO NOT

- Give the patient alcohol (absolutely NOT).
- Apply a tourniquet.
- Cut "X" marks about the bite holes, or attempt to suck out the venom. Snake venom spreads quickly and efficiently through the lymphatic system (it is believed).
- Give the patient aspirin, ibuprofen, or any substance that would thin the blood.
- Expose the area of the bite to cold or to ice packs.

In the application of first aid to a snakebite victim, I have no knowledge or opinion regarding giving the victim narcotics or marijuana to ease anxiety and the pain. It's your call and responsibility for the results.

Identification of the species of snake is important for proper treatment. Locate the snake. Cut off its head with a long-handled shovel, and bring the head to the medical facility. Knowledgeable medicos can identify the species and begin specific treatment, which usually consists of injection of antivenin and other measures.

CAUTION. Some folks are allergic to the antivenin and can develop severe reactions. Ensure that the medicos conduct a sensitivity test before administering the antivenin.

In summary, a venomous snake bite is a medical emergency and the patient needs prompt medical attention. Try to keep the patient calm and allow him/her to drink only water. Again, NO alcohol.

Lastly, there are mountain lions in the mountainous terrain. These animals can be dangerous if they feel threatened. A female with her kittens is especially dangerous. From what I've read, mountain lions generally attack from the rear. During my ghost towning ventures, I've seen two mountain lions—both bounded away. I've seen plenty of their tracks in the snow and around springs. I always carry a large-caliber pistol anytime I'm in such areas. If I should encounter one in a threatening scenario, I'd shoot it if I could. You can't outrun one of these cats if it's after you. If you see one, get into your vehicle and drive off. That's my best advice.

Clinton, CA
Date of Photograph: 11 October, 1998
Ghost Town Rating: 5
Road Condition Rating: 3

Tunnel Camp, NV
Date of Photograph: 13 November, 1999
Ghost Town Rating: 7
Road Condition Rating: 3

Villa de la Mina, TX
Date of Photograph: 12 July, 2013
Ghost Town Rating: 9
Road Condition Rating: 2

Bodie, CA
Date of Photograph: 1 August, 1981
Ghost Town Rating: 10
Road Condition Rating: 2

Techaiticup, NV
Date of Photograph: 21 October, 1997
Ghost Town Rating: 7
Road Condition Rating: 2

Sierra Nevada Mill, Keeler, CA
Date of Photograph: 1 December, 1990
Ghost Town Rating: 7
Road Condition Rating: 2

Cerro Gordo, CA
Date of Photograph: 1 February 1987
Ghost Town Rating: 8
Road Condition Rating: 4

Cook Bank Building, Rhyolite, NV
Date of Photograph: 10 November, 1998
Ghost Town Rating: 9
Road Condition Rating: 1

Chapter Fourteen

What's Next

No matter how hard you've tried, your vehicle is stuck solid or has broken down, and you cannot get unstuck or repair the vehicle. Naturally, you don't have a second vehicle to push, pull, or winch your vehicle to firmer ground. Or, you don't have a winch, or anything to hook a winch onto. And, sure enough, you don't have a mountain bicycle or an all-terrain vehicle to get you to civilization and help. What's next?

Determine if you're in just an annoying situation or in a serious one. If it's annoyance, take appropriate measures to remedy the situation—usually a short walk to a major road or civilization to get help. If it's serious, timely and appropriate action is essential. First, let's determine what is "serious." You are:

- Deep in the boondocks
- Far from civilization
- Way off the beaten track
- The weather is very hot or cold
- It's late in the day
- Someone in your party has a medical emergency
- Your vehicle is inoperative (rollover or the like)

If your cellular telephone works, call the operator, sheriff, highway patrol, etc. Let them know your situation and find out when they'll get to you. Take life easy until help arrives. No need to expend energy and body fluids (water) unnecessarily. Sometimes when in the boondocks or in a steep canyon, a cellular telephone won't work. Walk uphill or out of the canyon and try again.

If your cellular telephone does not work, try with your satellite telephone.

Should neither telephone work, use your Citizen's Band (CB) radio and broadcast a MAY DAY on channel nine (9). Say in a calm, natural voice: "MAY DAY, MAY DAY, MAY DAY." Listen for a response for one minute. Repeat your MAY DAY transmissions for an hour or so. If no response, wait a couple of hours and try again. Varying atmospheric conditions affect CB transmissions. Should you get a response, tell the other person your name, location, type of help needed, and if you have a medical emergency. Unfortunately, the CB has a limited range and it is not very effective in deep canyons. Try other channels. In particular, try the channel the truckers use in your area. Walk to the crest of the hill to increase your range. Keep trying.

Should the Citizen's Band radio not work, what's next? Not to worry. Naturally, you've told some responsible person where you're going today and when to expect you back. And if you're not back within a couple of hours or so of your expected time of arrival (ETA), then they'll call appropriate authorities to find you—sheriff, highway patrol, local police, fire department, desert/mountain rescue group, etc.

Of course, if you are not stuck and you return within the ETA period, you always check in with the person you have told of your plans for the day telling them that you've returned.

Let's just suppose, for the sake of discussion, that you didn't discuss your plans for the day. Thus, you can't expect anyone to come looking for you. What's next?

There are no pat or easy answers. You could be in a tough situation. Cool, calm, collected, and rational thought and action are essential. The question is, should you attempt to walk out or stay with the vehicle? There are many factors to consider.

To Go or Not to Go

Should you be in a situation in which you must decide to stay with your vehicle or walk out, consider the following factors. I listed them in a general order of importance. It's GO or NO GO. Or perhaps, wait until the weather improves (naturally, you're getting weather reports over your battery-powered radio, cell phone, etc).

Carl Austin says, "The only reasons for leaving a vehicle are if you are sure you will not be looked for or if someone in your party is hurt seriously." (See Bibliography for details.)

Realize that you can't stay with the vehicle indefinitely. You'll run out of water and food. Of course, if you're in a well-traveled area, odds are in your favor that someone will drive by and render assistance within a day or so. If you're stuck in some corner of the boondocks, with little chance of help passing by, and know for sure that no one is looking for you, then you'll probably have to walk out. And the sooner you start the better. You'll be in better physical and mental condition and you'll have more water.

Distance to Help
- How far is it to help in terms of miles and time?
- Do you know exactly where you want to go?
- What are the odds of you, or someone in your party, reaching help?

It's a risk/reward decision. Naturally, you zeroed your trip odometer as you left the main road so you know how far you've traveled and how far you have to go back to the good road/civilization.

Should you decide to walk out, the most important action you should take is to leave a note secured firmly on the dashboard. Note the date and time you left, direction of travel ("north by northwest," or "toward the high peak at the end of the valley to the South"). Describe your physical and mental condition—for example "I've taken the last of my heart medicine." List the names and phone numbers of several people who know you well and are familiar with your ongoing physical condition.

Make an arrow with rocks pointing to your direction of travel. Use the 1:24K maps to plot your course. Take the maps and track your course with the topographic information on the maps. On average, over a smooth and flat surface (sidewalk, for example), a moderate walking pace is about two miles per hour. Walk moderately for about 30 minutes, then take a 10- to 15-minute rest. Rest in the shade, if found nearby, and off the ground if possible. Ground temperature can be twenty degrees hotter than the air temperature. Continue this walk/rest cycle until fatigue begins to be a telling factor. As you tire, take longer breaks.

What to Take
- Take as much water as possible.
- The revolver and ammunition

- Pen and paper
- Signaling equipment
- GPS device
- Enough other survival equipment to get the odds of success in your favor

Don't overdo it, however. Too much weight will bog you down on a long trek. If you realize that you can't make it to help during the day you start, take appropriate material (blanket, etc.) to bed down for the night.

As you walk, leave notes in obvious places along your track. Include name, physical condition, date, time, direction of travel, expected end. Do this every hour or so.

Weather conditions

Hot, cold, moderate, snowing, hailing, raining. If it's blistering hot or numbing cold, consider staying with the vehicle for a time until conditions improve. Get weather reports over your portable radio. If you go, dress appropriately. Realize your endurance in such conditions is reduced significantly.

Your physical conditions/health

Injured (serious or moderate), overall fitness. The question is: Can you make it? The last thing you want to happen is for you to collapse somewhere between your vehicle and help.

Mental Condition

Mindset, resolve, mental toughness. Do you have the wherewithal to complete the trip—no matter what?
Physical/mental condition of others in your party. Does anyone in the party require medical attention? Immediately? Give appropriate first aid. Notwithstanding your party's medical needs, don't make a hasty or imprudent decision.

Difficulty of the walk itself

Up steep grades? In deep sand, snow, ice, etc.? As a rule, it's best to walk downhill and to follow trails and roads, streams, gullies, telephone/power lines, and pipelines—anything man-made that will lead you to civilization. Cutting cross-country generally is ill-advised. Such an action might be OK if you're positive that help is much closer by this route, or if you know it's a very long way around the "other" way.

Water

How much water do you have and how much can you carry? Water weighs about two pounds per quart—eight pounds per gallon. On average, in midsummer, with moderate activity, a person needs from three quarts to a gallon per day. Don't ration water. Drink as you need it. On the whole, it's best to maintain maximum fitness and strength as long as possible. In moderate and cold climes, one's water needs naturally are less. But don't be deceived. You'll still need lots of water. In the winter, water should be much more available: ice, snow, etc.

Food

Don't eat if it's hot. It takes too much of your body fluids (water) to process the food. You can survive for a long time (20 days or more) without food. But you can survive only a few days without water. If it's cold, eat. You need calories to maintain strength.

Time of day

It's best to start and complete your walk in daylight. Twilight and early sunrise are excellent times to walk. Though there's disagreement about nighttime walking in the desert, I suggest that it's best not to because there are too many hazards: boulders, mine shafts, cliffs, and rattlesnakes. In particular, don't walk on paved or smooth gravel roads at night. This is where rattlesnakes congregate to soak up the warmth that such roads radiate. I recall that one late night we were traveling on a small paved road deep in the Mojave Desert. Within several miles, we counted fifty-one rattlesnakes on the road. If you must walk at night, use your wide-beam, battery-powered lantern to scan the road in front and to the sides. A nighttime walk is more efficient in terms of water expenditure. One gets several more miles per gallon of water in the cooler nighttime.

Spend the night

If your trek is too far to complete in one day, then it's time to shut down and try again tomorrow. Bed down on sand or in a wash to avoid the wind. CAUTION. Stay out of washes in wet weather. A flash flood will ruin your evening. Or make your own shelter with rocks, branches, timbers, etc. Some experts advise us to avoid sheltering in a cave, overhang, mine entrance, shack, or rock outcropping, because creepy-crawly things and critters tend to inhabit such areas. Build a fire if feasible. Use all precautions and safety procedures. Don't burn up the forest or desert.

Let's go back to our GO, NO GO factors discussion. You've decided it's prudent to stay with the vehicle—for a time anyway. Naturally, you have lots of water and groceries, blankets, and all the other survival gear. In any case, don't delay starting to walk out beyond three days or wait until your water supply is down to less than three gallons—about the amount you can reasonably carry. What's next?

It's time to reflect and develop a plan. The primary question is: How long can you and your party remain with the vehicle before supplies are exhausted and you don't have enough for at least one of you to walk out? Three or four days, I would suggest, are maximum. Much of the information I've outlined in our GO scenario is applicable also.

Make a camp. Use the tarpaulin and tent pegs to make a lean-to. Don't expend energy and body fluids in frivolous pursuits. Conserve all resources.

Set up a watch schedule so that someone is awake and watchful at all times. A watch usually is about four hours long. Adjust the schedule to the capabilities of the persons in your party. All able-bodied persons will participate.

Your primary goal is to attract attention: passing airplanes, forest ranger, rancher, etc. Here are just a few of the strategies.

- **Flash the signaling mirror** at anything that moves: airplanes, cloud of dust (could be a vehicle on a dirt road), a glint (no matter how faint). The mirror's flash can be seen for miles. Know how to send an "SOS" with the mirror.

- **Light flares** if you hear mechanical noise. CAUTION. Be careful not to let the resultant effluent drop on you. It causes severe burns that are difficult to heal. And because you might start a brush or forest fire.

- **Lay out the survival bag** in a nearby clearing. Its bright orange color is eye-catching.

- **Make a large "SOS"** with rocks or shoveled sand close to your vehicle.

- **Make ground signals.** Contained in various survival books are ground signals for passing airplanes. These signals are made with rocks, tarpaulin, or orange survival bag. Consider making the letter "K." It should be about 12 feet long. "K" is a Vietnam–era military symbol that indicates a "friend is here and needs help." Be sure to destroy all ground signals when abandoning the camp or after being rescued.

- **Light several bonfires** in the shape of a triangle in the evening. Distance between the bonfires ought to be about 15 feet. Again, take precautions not to burn up the desert or your camp.

• **Burn things** to attract attention. Gasoline-soaked sagebrush and greasewood make lots and lots of smoke. Tires also make lots of smoke. Start with the spare. Be sure to start your fires downwind from your vehicle/camp. Take precautions not to start a brush/forest fire.

• **Burn the vehicle** when you've decided that your situation is desperate and it's your last resort. If possible, wait a day to see if you've attracted attention. If not, start hiking.

NEVER use these survival signals to play games, to fool someone, or to be a smart aleck. You could cause serious injury to rescue personnel, and such conduct smacks of the "cry wolf" syndrome. And you just might get into serious trouble with the authorities.

Clearly, in this short discussion, I did not cover all options of the GO, NO GO scenario. I urge you to further your survival education before venturing too far into the boondocks by attending survival class, through additional in-depth reading, and by being prepared mentally and physically. And as a last comment: Never start a ghost town trip without having a detailed plan, maps, and survival gear. Don't take foolish risks.

Have a great time exploring and photographing the wonders of the historic sites in the West.

Tunnel Camp, NV
Date of Photograph: 13 November, 1989
Ghost Town Rating: 7
Road Condition Rating: 3

General store, Katemcy, TX
Date of Photograph: 31 July, 2011
Ghost Town Rating: 5
Road Condition Rating: 1

Terlingua, TX
Date of Photograph: 30 July, 2010
Ghost Town Rating: 7
Road Condition Rating: 1

Salt Mill, Parran, NV
Date of Photograph: 13 October, 1998
Ghost Town Rating: 2
Road Condition Rating: 2

Cord Mill, NV
Date of Photograph: 5 March, 1998
Ghost Town Rating: 6
Road Condition Rating: 3

Murphy Mine and Mill, Ophir, NV
Date of Photograph: 5 November, 1992
Ghost Town Rating: 8
Road Condition Rating: 5

Paradise Valley, NV
Date of Photograph: 10 June, 2000
Ghost Town Rating: 8
Road Condition Rating: 1

Stage Coach Station, Tybo to Eureka, Moores Station, NV
Date of Photograph: 29 October, 1993
Ghost Town Rating: 8
Road Condition Rating: 2

CHAPTER FIFTEEN

VERITIES OF GHOST TOWNING

Over the many years I've spent ghost towning in the West, I've begun to realize that there are fundamental realities that suffuse throughout the area. They are inviolate, immutable, and inerrant. Here's my list of such verities that I've experienced—firsthand.

1. The next site is always just around the bend in the road.
2. No matter how far you hike up the mountain, the site is always over the next rise.
3. The map you need to find that outstanding site is back in the motel room.
4. Even though you don't see the mountain lion, he sees you.
5. The more remote and inaccessible the narrow mountain trail, the more likely you'll meet another vehicle coming the other way.
6. As you come to the washout on the narrow, steep, four-wheel-drive trail, the "turn around" always is "way back there."
7. On returning to the unlocked gate that you opened a short time ago to get to that fabulous site, you'll find that the gate now is locked.
8. As you approach the intersection in the remote outback, suddenly a rapidly moving truck will appear on the crossroad just in front of you.
9. The rock you don't see is the rock on which you'll high center.
10. The farther from civilization, the more likely it is that your vehicle will break down.
11. The spare tire is always flat.
12. The more luxurious the road, the more likely you've forgotten to take the vehicle out of four-wheel drive.
13. The gasoline gauge lies!
14. The ol' timer's directions to the forgotten site are pithy, revealing, and wrong.
15. The GPS lies!
16. The more film you bring, the faster you'll run out, or no matter how many batteries you bring, they'll all be dead.
17. The black & white filter is always on the lens.
18. That town up the road has three casinos, but it doesn't have a service station.
19. The more difficult it is to get to the site, the better the odds are that the sun will cloud over on arrival.
20. A bright sunny morning at the motel guarantees snow at the most desirable site—which is usually up a steep, four-wheel drive, mountain canyon.
21. The farther you travel up the box canyon, the farther back is the turnaround.

22. The map lies!

23. Trusting a local citizen for directions guarantees that you'll get lost.

24. Even on the hottest summer day, the only road to the site will be washed out by snowmelt runoff.

25. When estimating travel times, multiply by two and add the square root of the wind velocity.

26. Flashlight batteries always are dead.

27. On arriving at that great site, several miles up the box canyon, you realize that you've left the coffeepot on back in the motel room.

28. Regardless of the number of wild animals sighted during a trip, your partner always has seen more on a previous trip.

29. The smoother the dirt road and the higher your vehicle's speed, the odds increase exponentially that you won't see the washout.

30. As the afternoon wanes, squeezing in a photographic visit to the last site listed on the schedule guarantees that the site will be in shade in an east-facing box canyon.

31. The next site always is the "best" site.

32. The cell phone will not work in the box canyon.

33. The lower the fuel gauge, the higher the probability is that the only service station in the next town is closed.

34. Notwithstanding the paucity of hard evidence, one can justify the location of a "lost" site by rationalizing that some miscellaneous junk spotted in the general area is the remains of the site.

Villa de la Mina, TX
Date of Photograph: 12 July, 2013
Ghost Town Rating: 9
Road Condition Rating: 2

Bonanza Trail, CA
Date of Photograph: 18 October, 2001
Ghost Town Rating: 3
Road Condition Rating: 3

Schoolhouse, Rhyolite, NV
Date of Photograph: 10 November, 1991
Ghost Town Rating: 9
Road Condition Rating: 1

Gold Processing Mill (in background, seen from the saw mill), Bodie, CA
Date of Photograph: 1 August, 1981
Ghost Town Rating: 10
Road Condition Rating: 2

Moapa, NV
Date of Photograph: 28 October, 2007
Ghost Town Rating: 7
Road Condition Rating: 2

Pat Reddy's House, Bodie, CA
Date of Photograph: 1 August, 1981
Ghost Town Rating: 10
Road Condition Rating: 2

Opera House, Hamilton, NV
Date of Photograph: 23 October, 1994
Ghost Town Rating: 8
Road Condition Rating: 3

Cow Camp, Hyde Well, NV
Date of Photograph: 7 November, 1990
Ghost Town Rating: 5
Road Condition Rating: 3

CHAPTER SIXTEEN

PHOTOGRAPHIC COLLECTION DONATION

Over fourteen years, Captain S. Martin Shelton, USNR (ret.) made 39 trips into Nevada to discover and document with color slides and black and white photography some 1,400 historic sites in the state. Though exact figures are not available, experts estimate that he has photographed at least 99 percent of all sites in Nevada. Shelton built a database of all these sites, including site name, location in latitude and longitude, alternate names, descriptions, road conditions, topographic maps needed, and other information.

In October 2003, Shelton contributed his photographic collection and ephemera to the state of Nevada through the Office of Historic Preservation. The collection consists of 6,639 color Kodachrome® slides, and 2,500 black and white, 8" x 10" photographs of Nevada ghost towns and mining camps. Included in his donation was his database, several hundred topographic maps, Operation Plans (OPLANS), camera logs, etc.

In appreciation for this significant historical gift, the governor, Kenny C. Gunn, presented Captain Shelton with a letter of thanks that recognized his outstanding contribution to the history of Nevada. US Senator John Ensign sent a Senatorial Recognition honoring Capt. Shelton for his dedication to the history of Nevada. And, the Department of Cultural Affairs of Nevada, State Historic Preservation Office presented Captain Shelton with an award of recognition for his lasting contribution to Nevada.

In 2012, the Historic Preservation Office moved Shelton's donation to the University of Nevada's, Reno, Library in the Special Collections section. With prearranged permission, serious researchers may view the collection. Captain Shelton visited the University of Nevada's Special Collections section in October 2014. He found that the staff was working diligently to catalog and store his collection.

Betty O'Neal Mine, NV
Date of Photograph: 18 November, 2000
Ghost Town Rating: 6
Road Condition Rating: 3

Withington Hotel, Hamilton, NV
Date of Photograph: 23 October, 1994
Ghost Town Rating: 8
Road Condition Rating: 3

Highbridge Mill, NV
Date of Photograph: 15 November, 1991
Ghost Town Rating: 5
Road Condition Rating: 3

Berlin, NV
Date of Photograph: 17 November, 1989
Ghost Town Rating: 8
Road Condition Rating: 2

Ludwick, NV
Date of Photograph: 11 September, 2002
Ghost Town Rating: 6
Road Condition Rating: 3

Belmont Mill, NV
Date of Photograph: 24 October, 1993
Ghost Town Rating: 7
Road Condition Rating: 4

Schoolhouse, Rhyolite, NV
Date of Photograph: 10 November, 1991
Ghost Town Rating: 9
Road Condition Rating: 2

Minerva, NV
Date of Photograph: 2 November, 1990
Ghost Town Rating: 7
Road Condition Rating: 2

CHAPTER SEVENTEEN

A POTPOURRI OF SCENIC PHOTOGRAPHS

While on your photographic ghost town trip, spot the beautiful scenes about you. Oftentimes it takes a critical eye to "see" the photograph. For example, the first photograph in this chapter is titled "Quaking Aspens."

Here's the story about this Quaking Aspens shot. It was mid-October, my ghost-town partner and I were traveling up a serious four-wheel road along San Juan Creek, in the Shoshone Mountains in central Nevada. Suddenly, we were surrounded by a copse of quaking aspen trees in their autumn glory. We stopped, I rolled down the window, stuck my camera out the open window, composed the shot, and squeezed the shutter release.

In fact, I took most of the photographs in this chapter in similar circumstances. Here's the challenge: keep your critical eye alert and your camera ready. Please enjoy the following scenes.

"Quaking Aspens," Shoshone Mountains, NV
Date of Photograph: 14 October, 1999

Guadalupe Mountains National Park, TX
Date of Photograph: 17 October, 2007

"Quaking Aspens," Siegel Creek, NV
Date of Photograph: 26 October, 1994

"Approaching Winter Storm," Highway 50, Big Smoky Valley, NV
Date of Photograph: 10 October, 2000

Coral Pink Sand Dunes State Park, UT
Date of Photograph: 27 September, 1992

"Pecan Trees," Jonah, TX
Date of Photograph: 29 April, 2004

Beowawe Cemetery, Eureka County, NV
Date of Photograph: 25 October, 2000

"My Blazer," Cottonwood Canyon, NV
Date of Photograph: 14 October, 1998

Onion Creek, Dripping Springs, TX
Date of Photograph: 1 April, 2005

Oasis Valley, Nye County, NV
Date of Photograph: 1 March, 1998

"Split-rail Fence," Fredericksburg, TX
Date of Photograph: 28 July, 2009

"Quaking Aspens," Paradise Range, NV
Date of Photograph: 17 November, 1989

"Wildflowers" at the Cotton Mill, Walberg, TX
Date of Photograph: 1 May, 1995

"Forest Home," Garden Valley, NV
Date of Photograph: 22 October, 1994

"Lone Cabin," Panguitch, UT
Date of Photograph: 26 September, 2002

"Red Door," Holland, TX
Date of Photograph: 1 May, 2005

BIBILOGRAPHY

Austin, Carl and Barbara, Common Sense in Desert Travel, Ridgecrest, Calif.: Maturango Museum, Inc., 1989, p. 36.

Broman, Mickey, Nevada Ghost Towns Trails, revised ed., Baldwin Park, California: Gem Guides Book Company, 1984, p. 80.

Brunner, Lillian Sholtis and Doris Smith Suddarth, The Lippincott Manual of Nursing Practice, 4th ed., Philadelphia: J. B. Lippincott Company, 1986, p. 1,562.

Cahill, Matthew, Editorial Director, Illustrated Manual of Nursing Practice, Springhouse, Pennsylvania: Springhouse Corporation, 1991, p. 1,459.

Carlson, Helen S., Nevada Place Names: A Geographical Dictionary, Reno, Nevada: University of Nevada Press, 1974, p. 282.

Davis, William C., Historic Site Studies in Churchill County, Nevada, Baltimore, American Library Press, Inc., 1998, p. 123.

Editor, Nevada Atlas & Gazetteer, first ed., Freeport, Maine: DeLorme, 1996, p. 72.

Fenstermaker-Danner, Ruth, Gabbs Valley, Nevada, Winnemucca, Nevada: Ruth Danner Publisher, 1992, pp. 416.

Florin, Lambert, Nevada Ghost Towns, Seattle: Superior Publishing Company, 1971, pp. 96.

Florin, Lambert, Ghost Towns of the West, New York, Promontory Press, 1970, pp. 872.

Fox, Theron, Nevada Treasure Hunters Ghost Town Guide, Las Vegas, Nevada: Nevada Publications, 1961, pp. 24.

Hall, Shawn R., A Guide to the Ghost Towns and Mining Camps of Nye County, Nevada, New York: Dodd, Mead & Company, 1981, pp. 162.

Hall, Shawn R., Old Heart of Nevada: Ghost Towns and Mining Camps of Elko County, Reno, Nevada: University of Nevada Press, 1998, pp. 308.

Hall, Shawn R., Romancing Nevada's Past: Ghost Towns and Historic Sites of Eureka, Lander, and White Pine Counties, Reno, Nevada: University of Nevada Press, 1994, pp. 226.

Headquarters, Department of the Army, U S Army Survival Manual, 9th ed., FM 21-76, New York: Dorset Press, 1988, p. 128.

Hensher, Alan, Ghost Towns of the Mojave Desert, Los Angeles: California Classic Books, 1991, pp. 63.

Jackson, W. Turrentine, Treasure Hill: Portrait of a Silver Mining Camp, Reno, Nevada: University of Nevada Press, 2000, p. 5.

Laskowski-Jones, RN, "Emergencies (in Warm-Weather Pursuits)," Nursing 2000, May 2000, pp. 35-39.

Lehman, Charles A., Desert Survival Handbook, 4th printing, Phoenix: Primer Publishers, 1993, p. 91.

McDowell, Jack, Supervising Editor, Ghost Towns of the West, revised ed., 1978, Menlo Park, California: Lane Publishing Company, p. 224.

Paher, Stan, Nevada Ghost Towns & Mining Camps, Volume One—Northern Nevada, Virginia City, Nevada: White Sage Studios, 1993, p. 103.

Paher, Stanley W., Nevada Ghost Towns & Mining Camps, Las Vegas, Nevada: Nevada Publications, 1984, p. 492.

Skrdla, Harry, Ghostly Ruins: America's Forgotten Architecture, New York, Princeton Architectural Press, 2006, pp. 222.

Varney, Philip, Ghost Towns of the Pacific Northwest, Minneapolis, Voyager Press, 2013, pp. 224.

Varney, Philip, Ghost Towns of California, Minneapolis, Voyager Press, 2012, pp. 240.

Varney, Philip, Ghost Towns of the Mountain West, Voyager Press, 2010, pp. 320.

Whisler, Kirk, publisher, Ghost Towns & Historic Sites Map, first edition, Carson City, Nevada: Nevada Magazine, 1987.

. ABOUT THE AUTHOR

Captain Shelton is retired from active and reserve U.S. Navy service. He attended the Naval School of Photography and documented Navy and Marine Corps activities in Korea, French Indochina, and other areas in the Western Pacific. Commissioned as a Photographic Officer, he then served in Vietnam and other Pacific regions.

Shelton earned his Master of Arts Degree (Cinema) at the University of Southern California. For thirty years, he produced a host of information and documentary motion-media shows, winning over forty awards in national and international film competitions and festivals. His peers elected him a Fellow of both the Information Film Producers of America and the Society for Technical Communication. He served as the President of the Information Film Producers of America.

He has published extensively in trade magazines, peer-reviewed journals, and commercial publications. His professional book, *Communicating Ideas with Film, Video, and Multimedia,* garnered the Best of Show award in the Society for Technical Communication's Spotlight Publication Competition.

Currently, he writes historical fiction and action-adventure novels whose *mise en scène* is the Far East and Africa. His first action-adventure novel, *St. Catherine's Crown,* published in 2013, was widely acclaimed by reviewers.

Details regarding his literary work are posted on Shelton's web site, **sheltoncomm.com**